Sports Illustrated KIDS
GRAPHIC NOVELS

STONE ARCH BOOKS
a capstone imprint

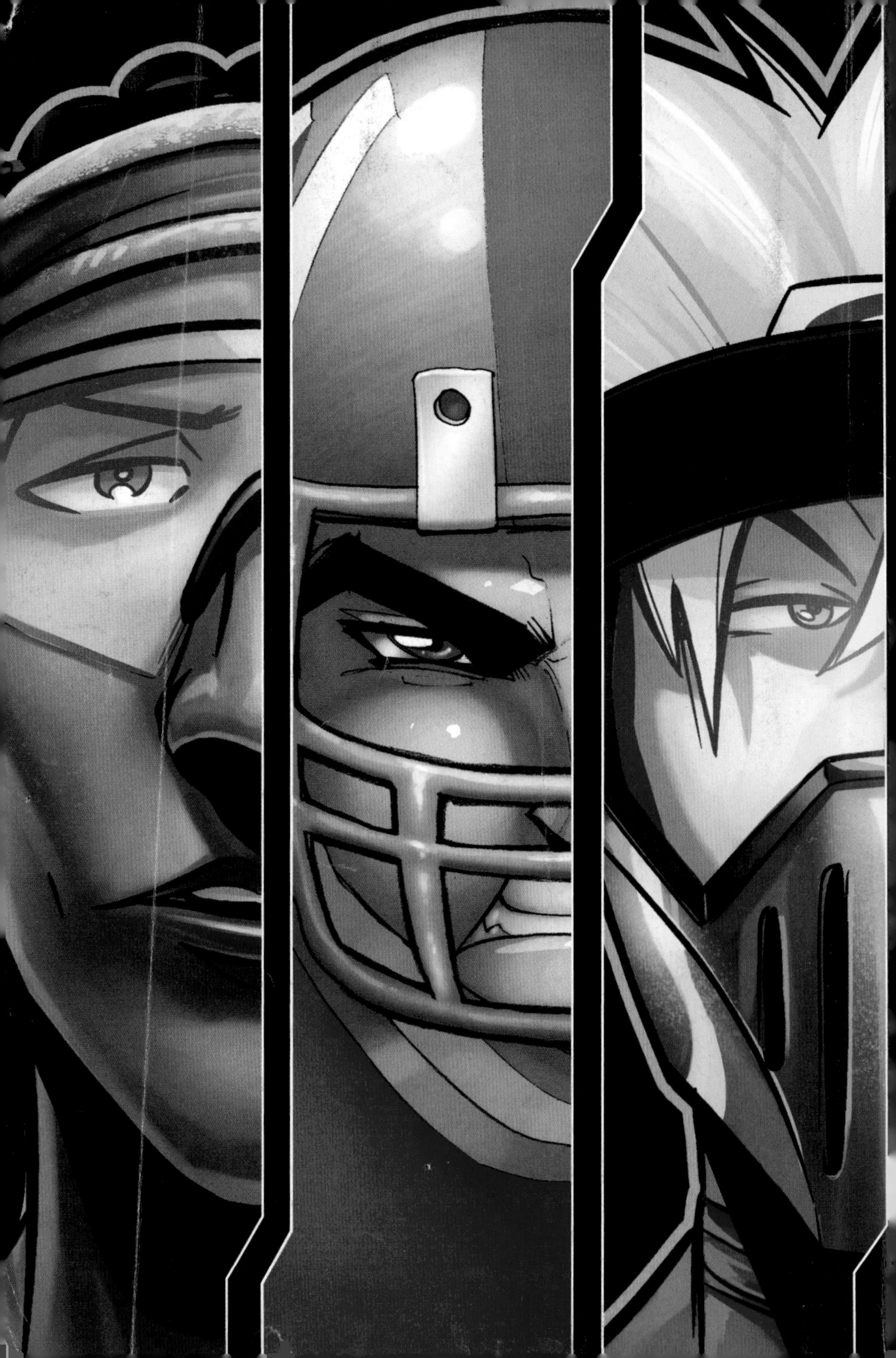

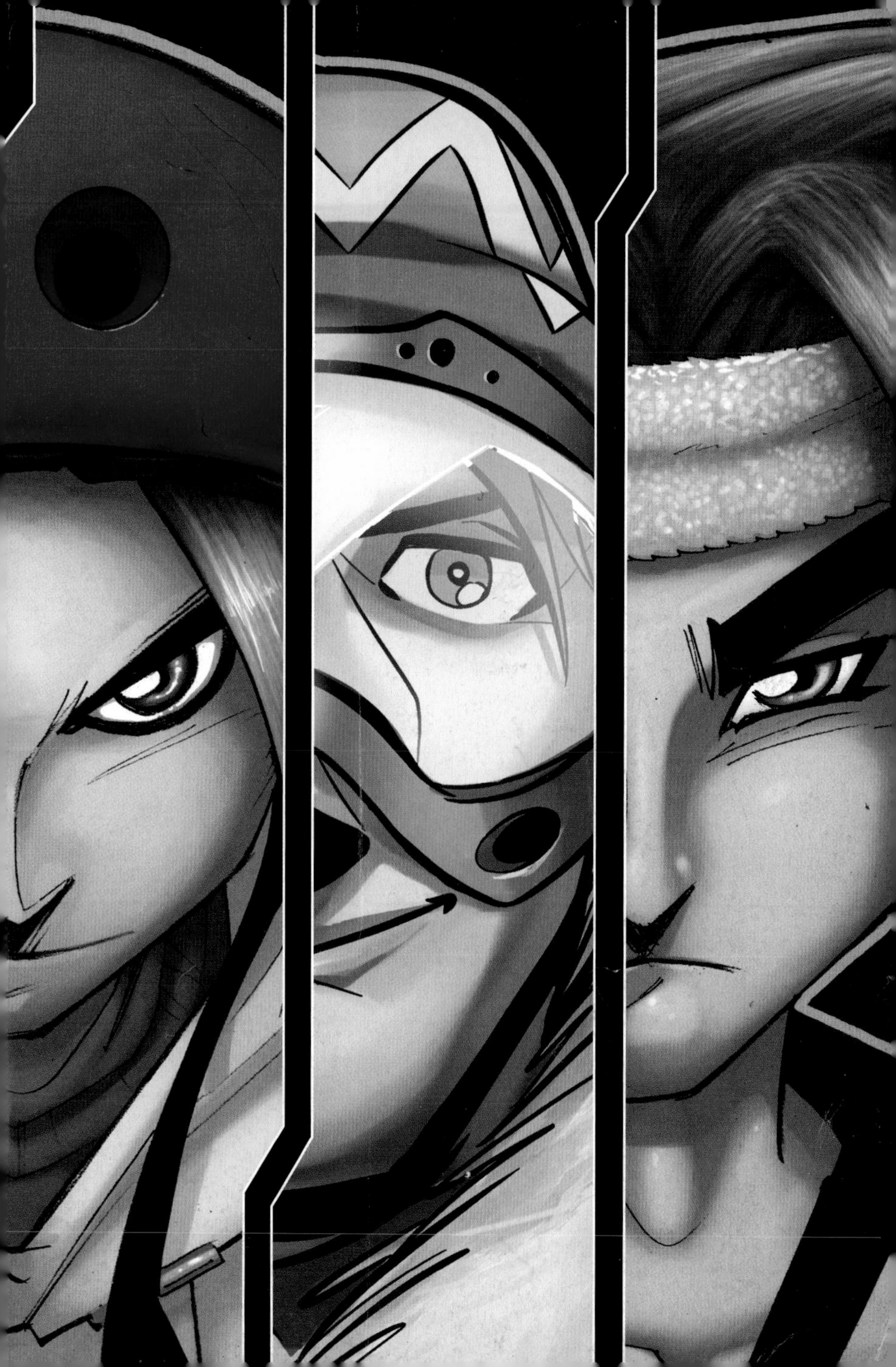

UP NEXT ›››

on Sports Illustrated KIDS

:02 SPORTS ZONE SPECIAL REPORT

:04 FEATURE PRESENTATION:

SHOT CLOCK SLAM

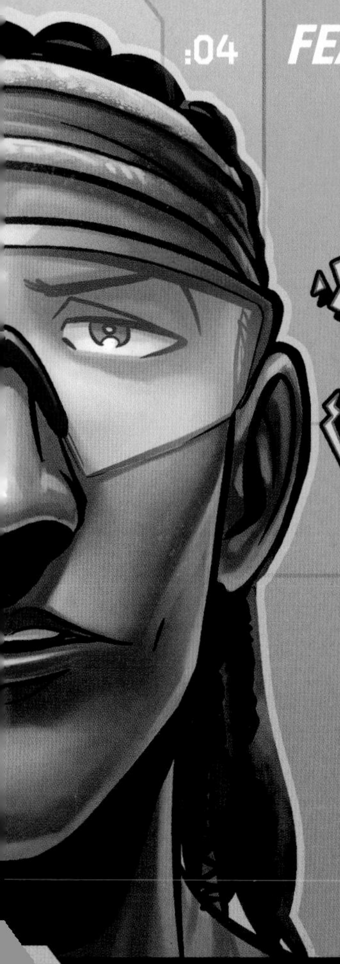

FOLLOWED BY:

:50 SPORTS ZONE POSTGAME RECAP

:51 SPORTS ZONE POSTGAME EXTRA

:52 SI KIDS INFO CENTER

TIGERS EXPECTED TO COMPETE FOR STATE TITLE THIS SEASON SIK TICKER

PORTS ZONE
CIAL REPORT

PERRY THE PLAYMAKER LOOKING TO LAUNCH THE TIGERS INTO FIRST PLACE

PERRY BOYD

STATS:
POSITION: GUARD
AGE: 14

BIO: Perry "Playmaker" Boyd is his team's best scorer and top go-to guy for all things offense. He has a lightning-fast crossover dribble, a quick release on his jumper, and he nails over 90 percent of his free throws. This playmaker only has one speed, and that's all-out, all the time. In fact, the only thing that can slow Perry down is his reluctance to involve others in the offense . . .

ports strated KIDS

UP NEXT: SHOT CLOCK SLAM

BLZ vs BKS 3-1
TGR vs RDR 33-32
EAG vs BAN 14-7
SPA vs WLD 4-3
BAN vs RDR 21-15
RZR vs LIG 4-3
BLZ vs BKS 3-1

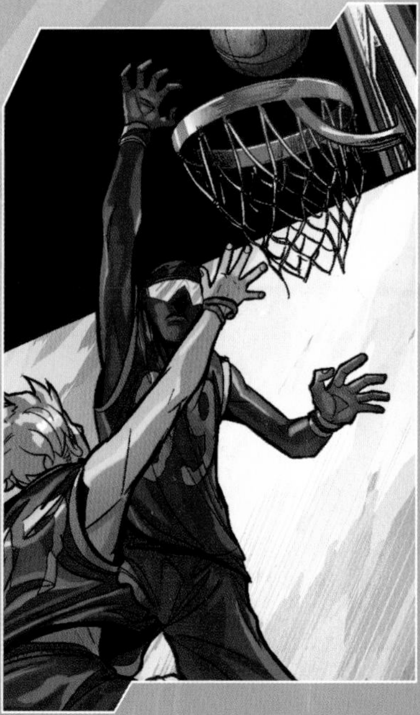

JASON CARTER

POSITION: CENTER

AGE: 14

BIO: Jason Carter used to be the same height as the rest of his classmates. But over this past year, Jason has grown six inches. Now, he towers over everyone — even his teachers.

KADIR AMAD

POSITION: POINT GUARD **AGE:** 14

BIO: Kadir is as quick as they come — his feet, and his mind, are lightning-fast . . . and his passes are even quicker!

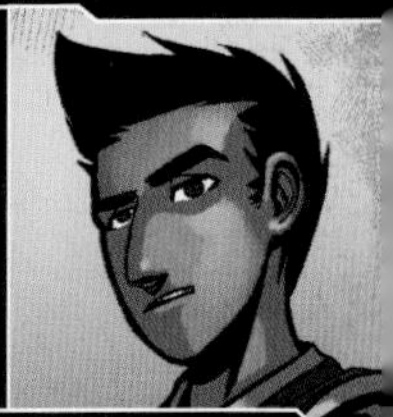

KADIR

COACH HECTOR

AGE: 37

BIO: Coach Hector knows how to get the best ouf of his players. He expects them to play hard, and practice even harder.

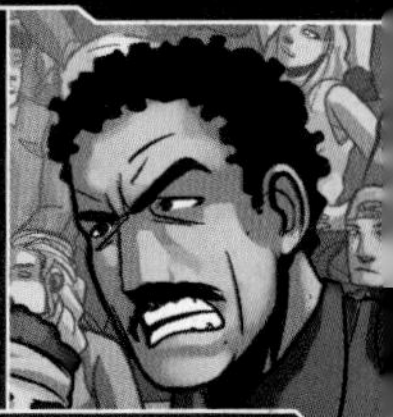

COACH

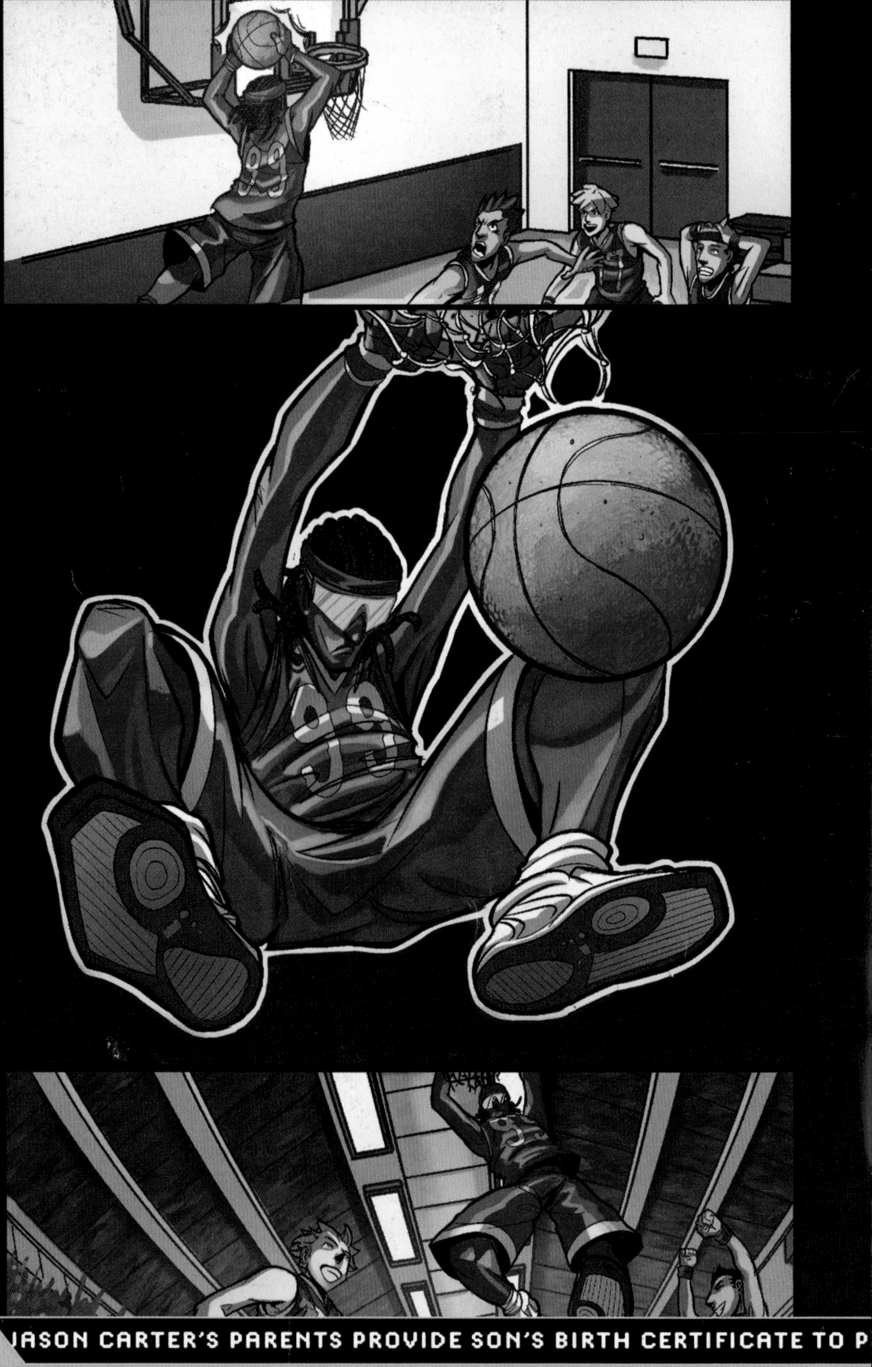
JASON CARTER'S PARENTS PROVIDE SON'S BIRTH CERTIFICATE TO P

Sports Illustrated KIDS

PRESENTS

SHOT CLOCK SLAM

A PRODUCTION OF

STONE ARCH BOOKS
a capstone imprint

written by Chris Kreie
illustrated by Aburtov
inked by Andres Esparza
colored by Fares Maese

designed and directed by Bob Lentz
edited by Sean Tulien
creative direction by Heather Kindseth
editorial direction by Michael Dahl

Sports Illustrated KIDS *Shot Clock Slam* is published by Stone Arch Books, 1710 Roe Crest Drive, North Mankato, Minnesota 56003.
www.capstonepub.com

Summary: Perry the Playmaker has always been the Tigers' go-to guy — until super-tall and ultra-talented Jason joins the team. Feeding the ball to Jason in the post is a guaranteed two points, but Perry refuses to play nice. Instead, he hogs the ball and takes bad shots, ruining the team's rhythm. Will Perry's selfishness spoil the Tigers' run at the state championship, or will the two talented teens team up to slam dunk the competition?

Cataloging-in-Publication Data is available at the Library of Congress website.

ISBN: 978-1-4342-2070-7 (library binding)
ISBN: 978-1-4342-2786-7 (paperback)

Printed in the United States of America in Stevens Point, Wisconsin.
072014 008385R

THAT JASON IS ONLY 14 DESPITE BEING OVER SIX FEET TALL SIK TICKER

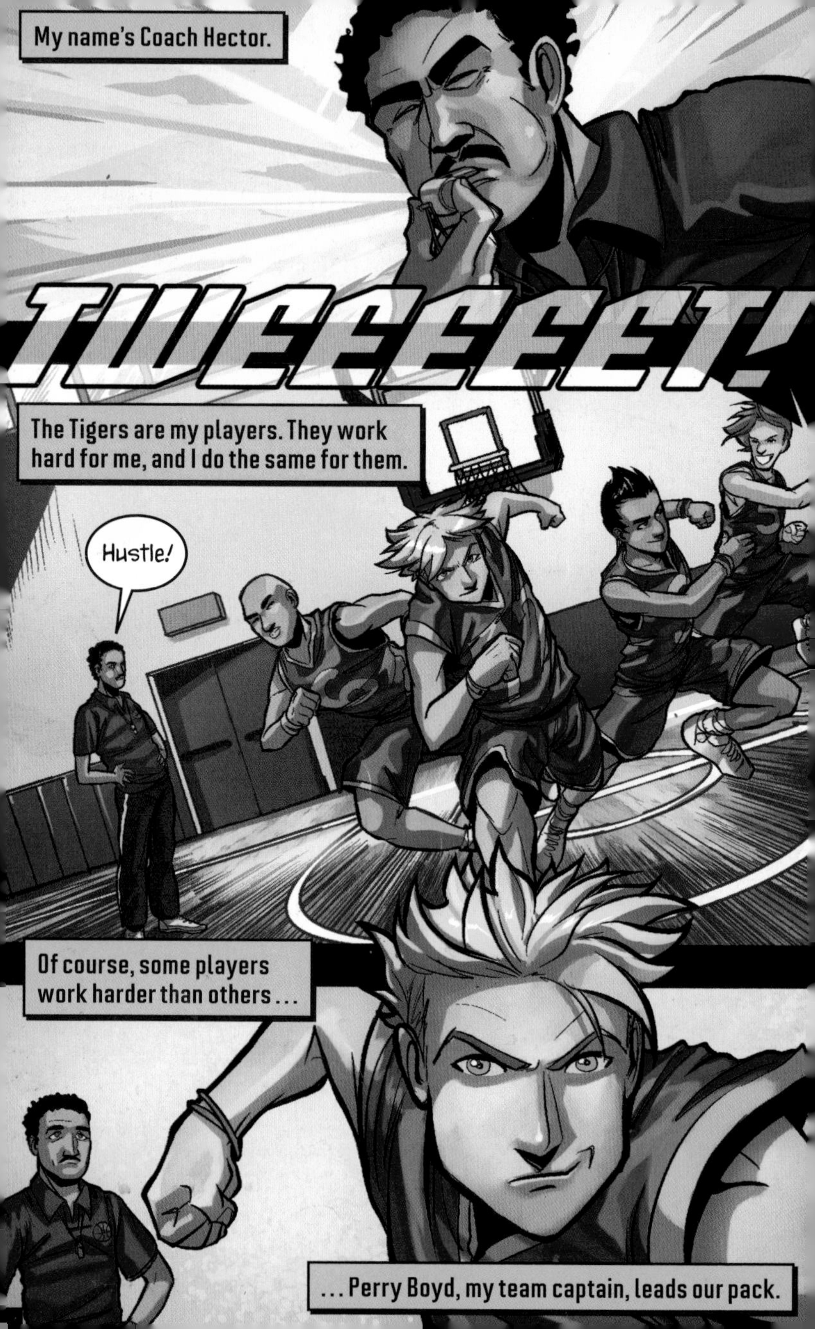
My name's Coach Hector.
TWEEEEET!
The Tigers are my players. They work hard for me, and I do the same for them.
Hustle!
Of course, some players work harder than others . . .
. . . Perry Boyd, my team captain, leads our pack.

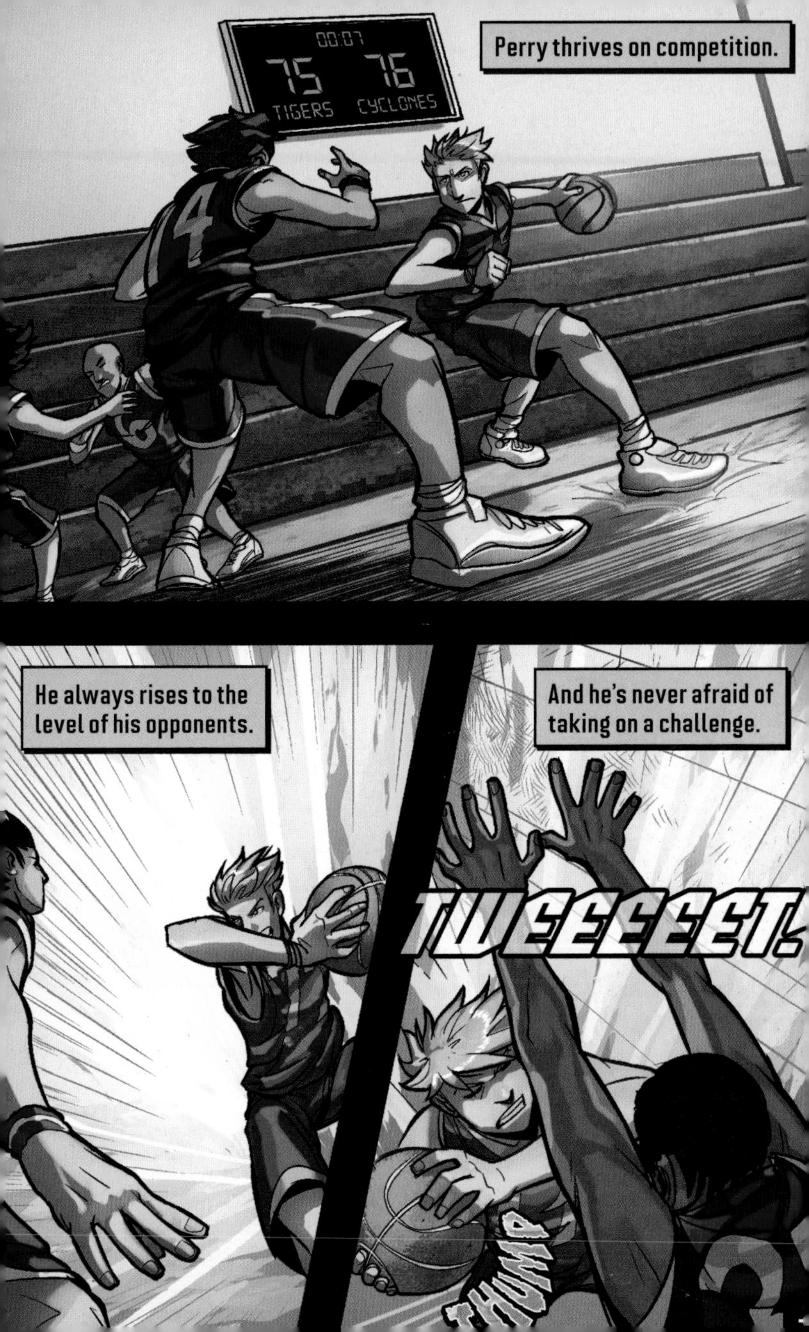
00:07
75
76
TIGERS
CYCLONES
Perry thrives on competition.
He always rises to the level of his opponents.
And he's never afraid of taking on a challenge.
TWEEEET.
THUMP

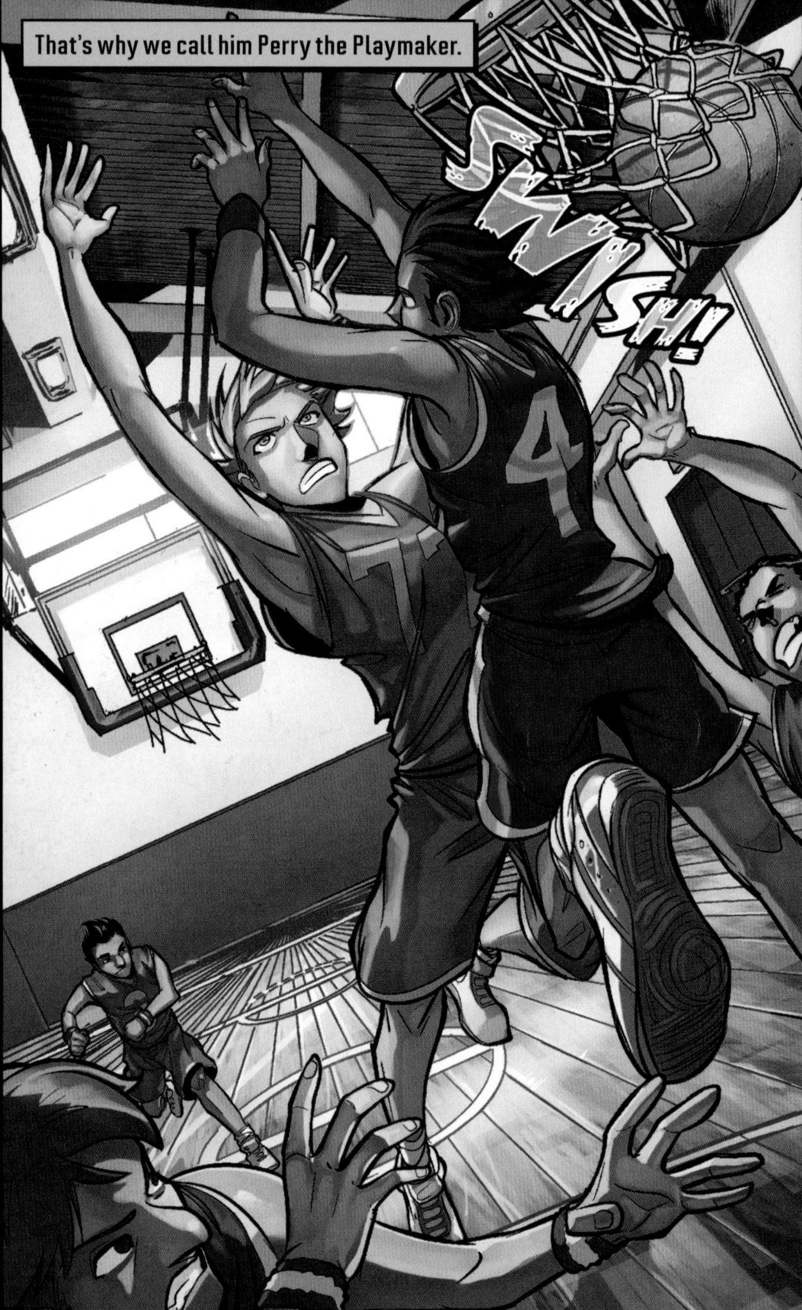
That's why we call him Perry the Playmaker.
SWISH!

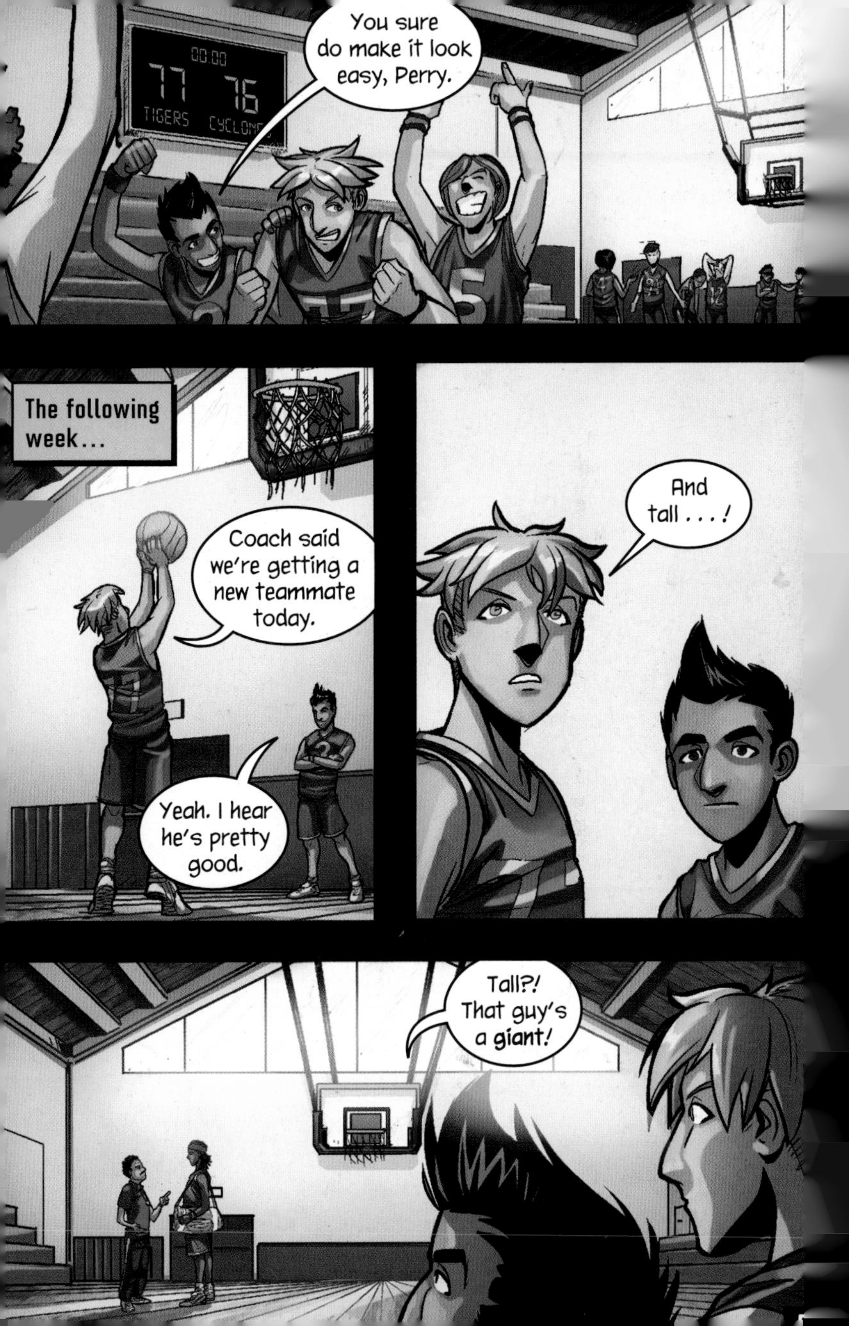
00:00
77 76
TIGERS CYCLONES
You sure do make it look easy, Perry.
The following week...
Coach said we're getting a new teammate today.
Yeah. I hear he's pretty good.
And tall . . . !
Tall?! That guy's a giant!

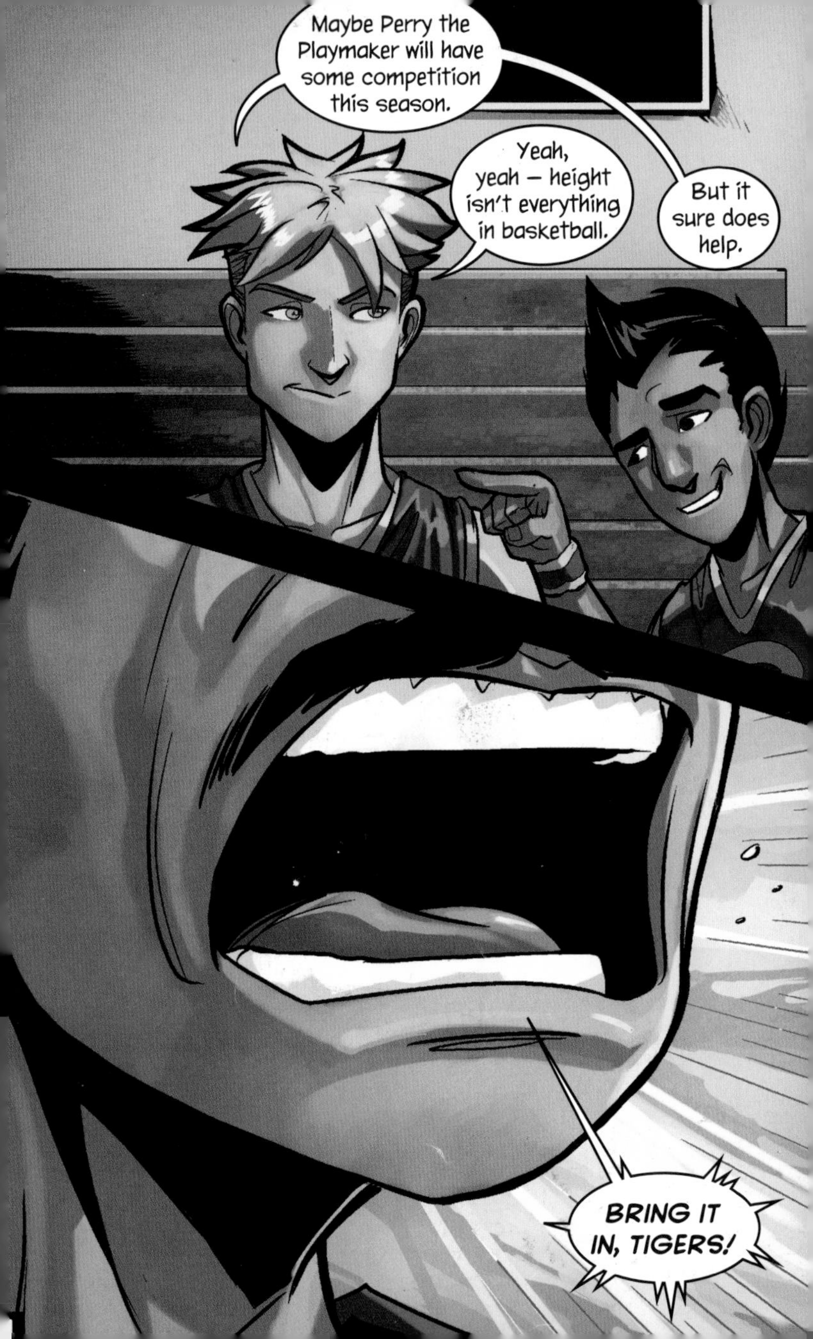
Maybe Perry the Playmaker will have some competition this season.
Yeah, yeah — height isn't everything in basketball.
But it sure does help.
BRING IT IN, TIGERS!

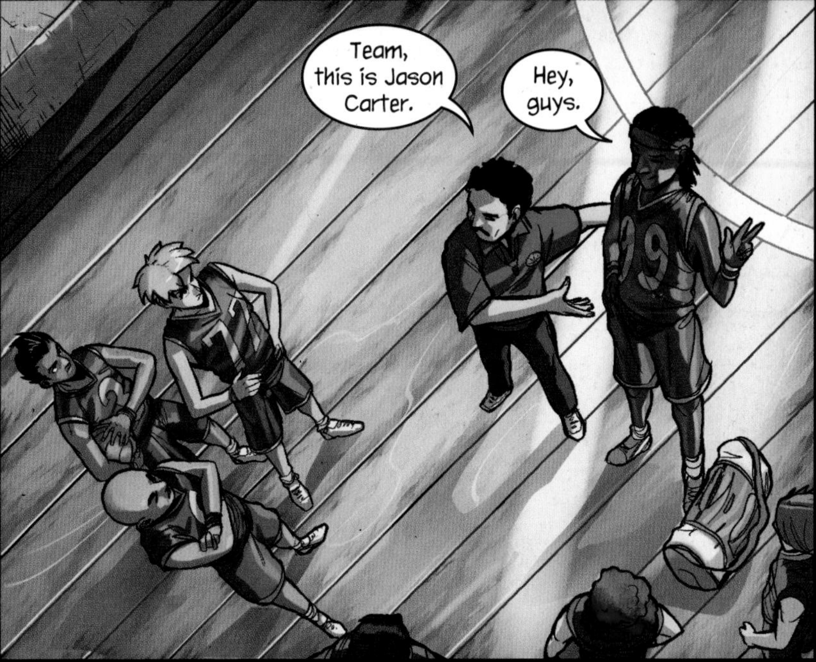
Team, this is Jason Carter.
Hey, guys.
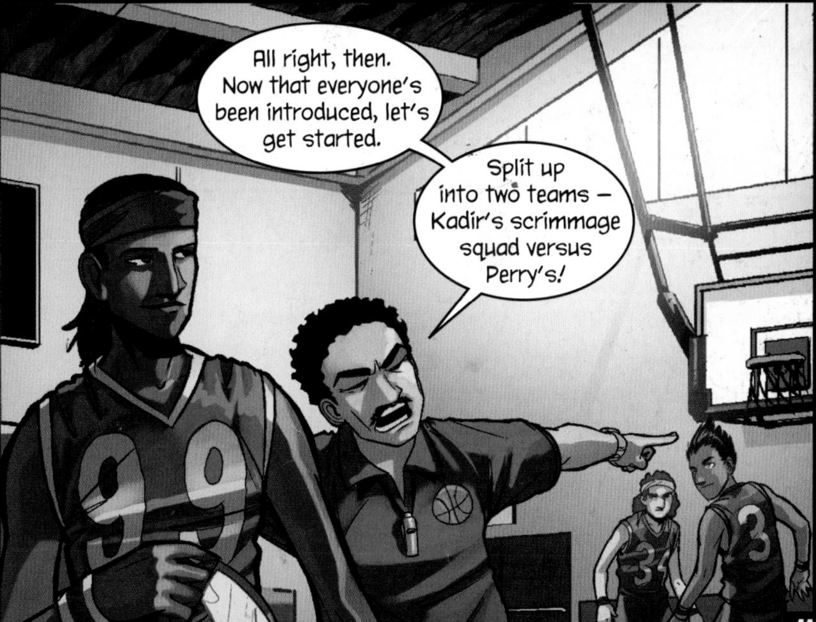
All right, then. Now that everyone's been introduced, let's get started.
Split up into two teams — Kadir's scrimmage squad versus Perry's!

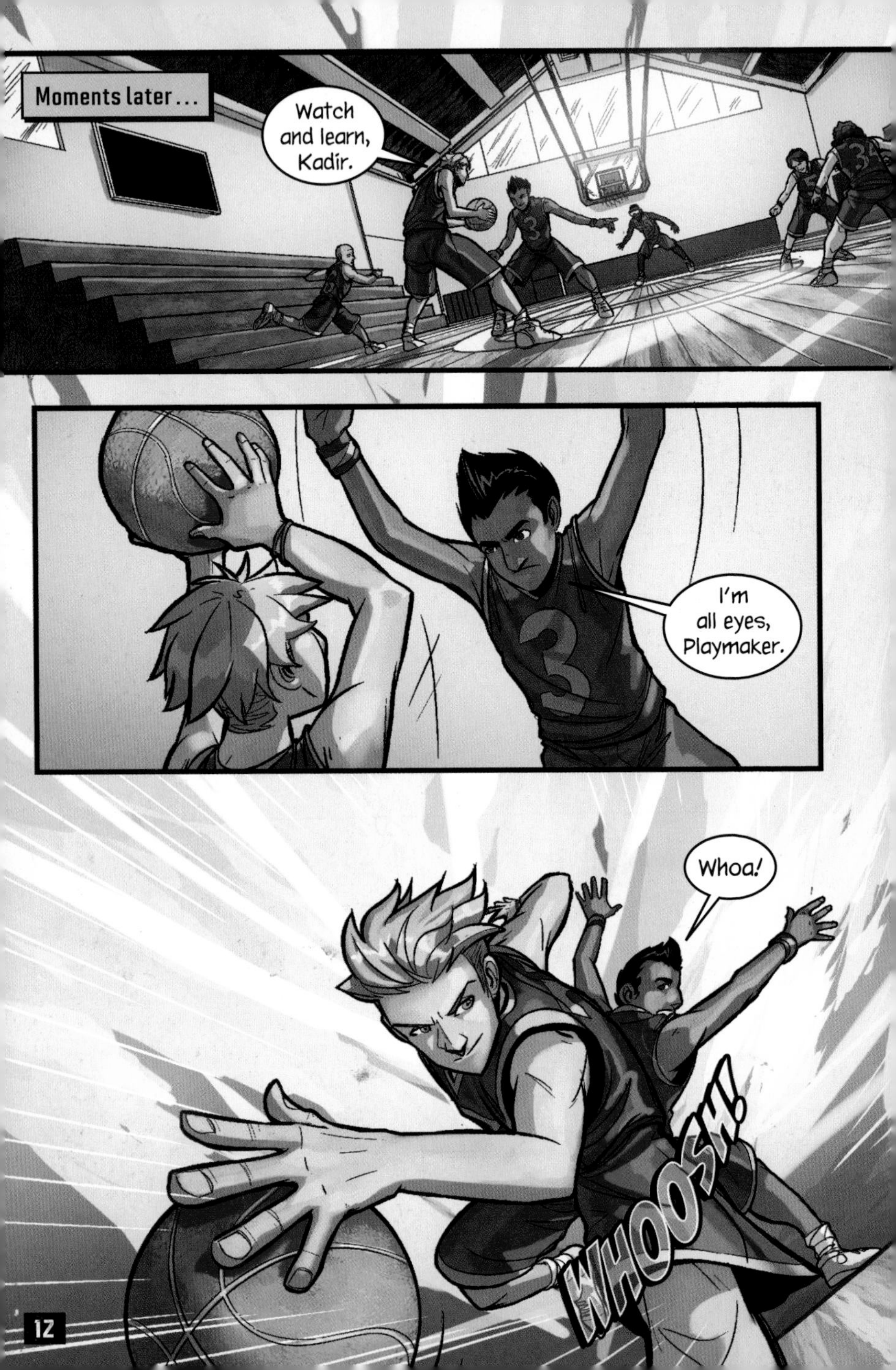
Moments later . . .
Watch and learn, Kadir.
I'm all eyes, Playmaker.
Whoa!
WHOOSH!

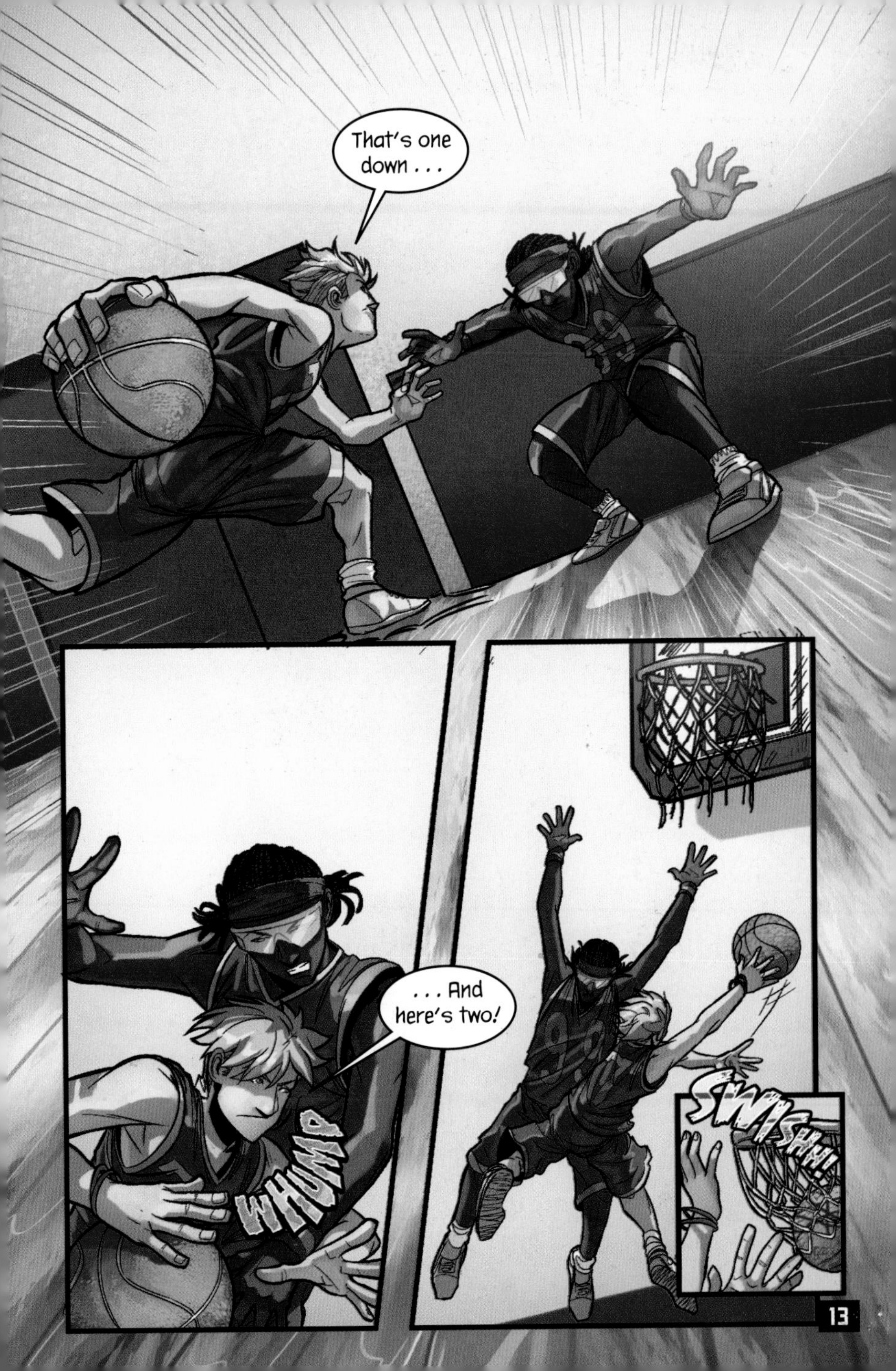
That's one down . . .
. . . And here's two!
WHUMP
SWISH!

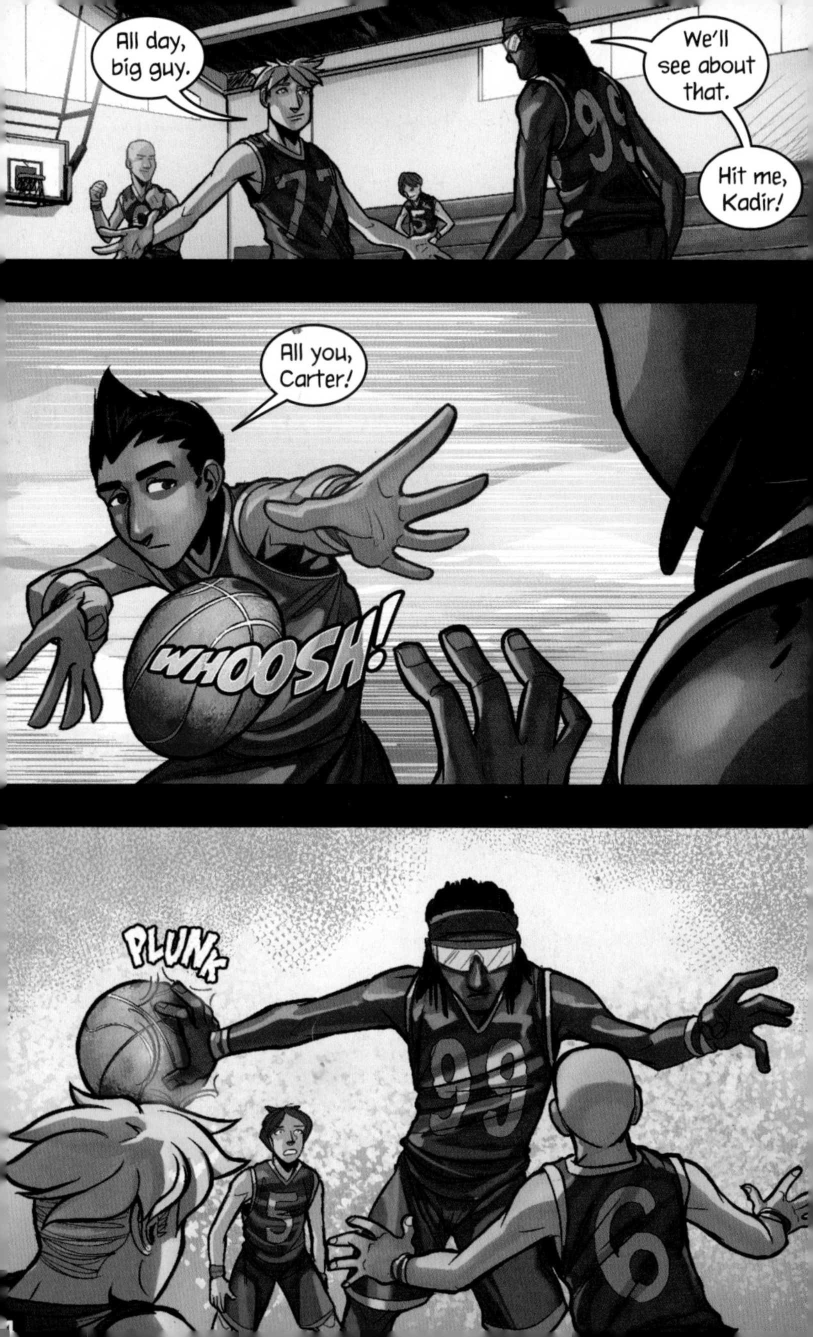
All day, big guy.
We'll see about that.
Hit me, Kadir!
All you, Carter!
WHOOSH!
PLUNK

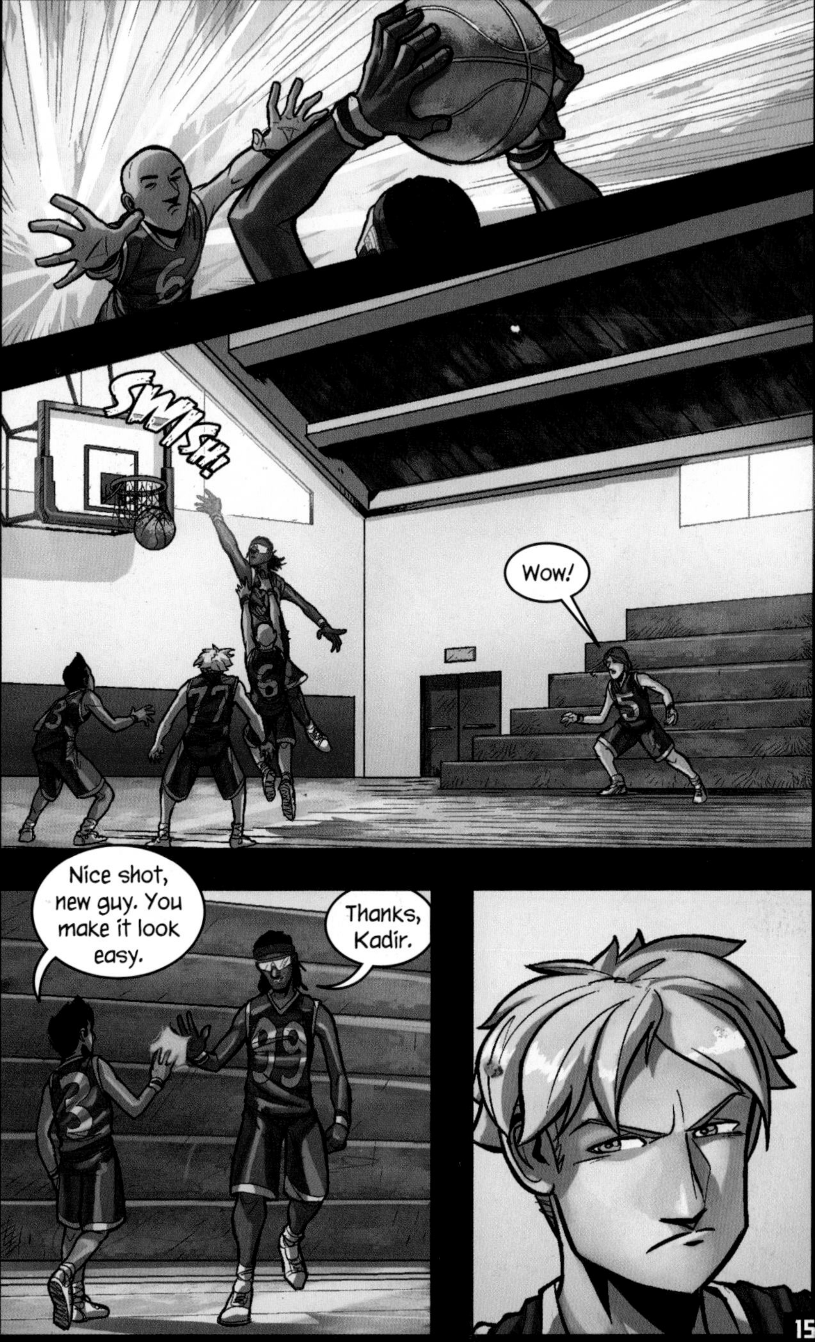
SWISH!
Wow!
Nice shot, new guy. You make it look easy.
Thanks, Kadir.

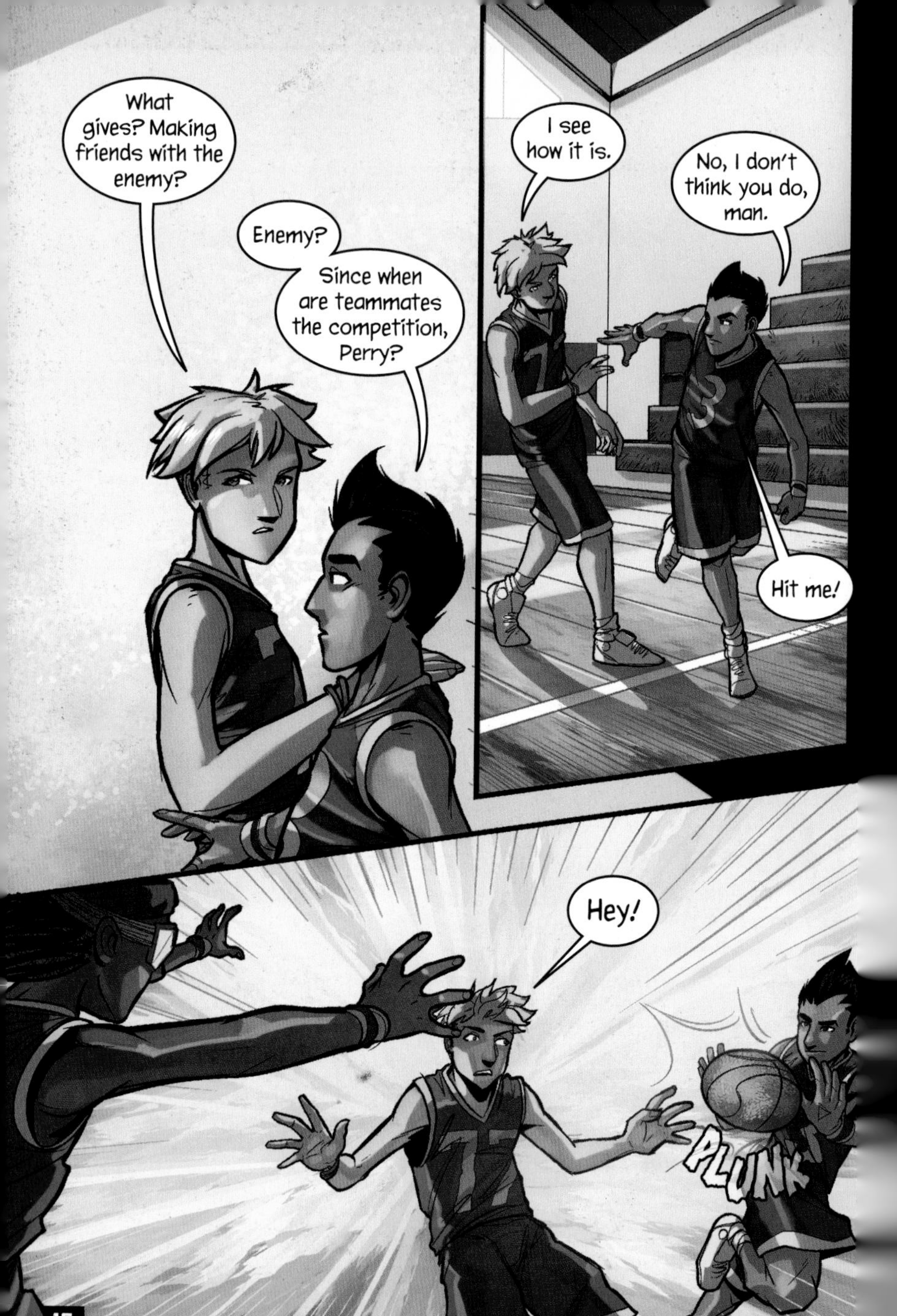

What gives? Making friends with the enemy?
Enemy?
Since when are teammates the competition, Perry?
I see how it is.
No, I don't think you do, man.
Hit me!
Hey!
PLUNK

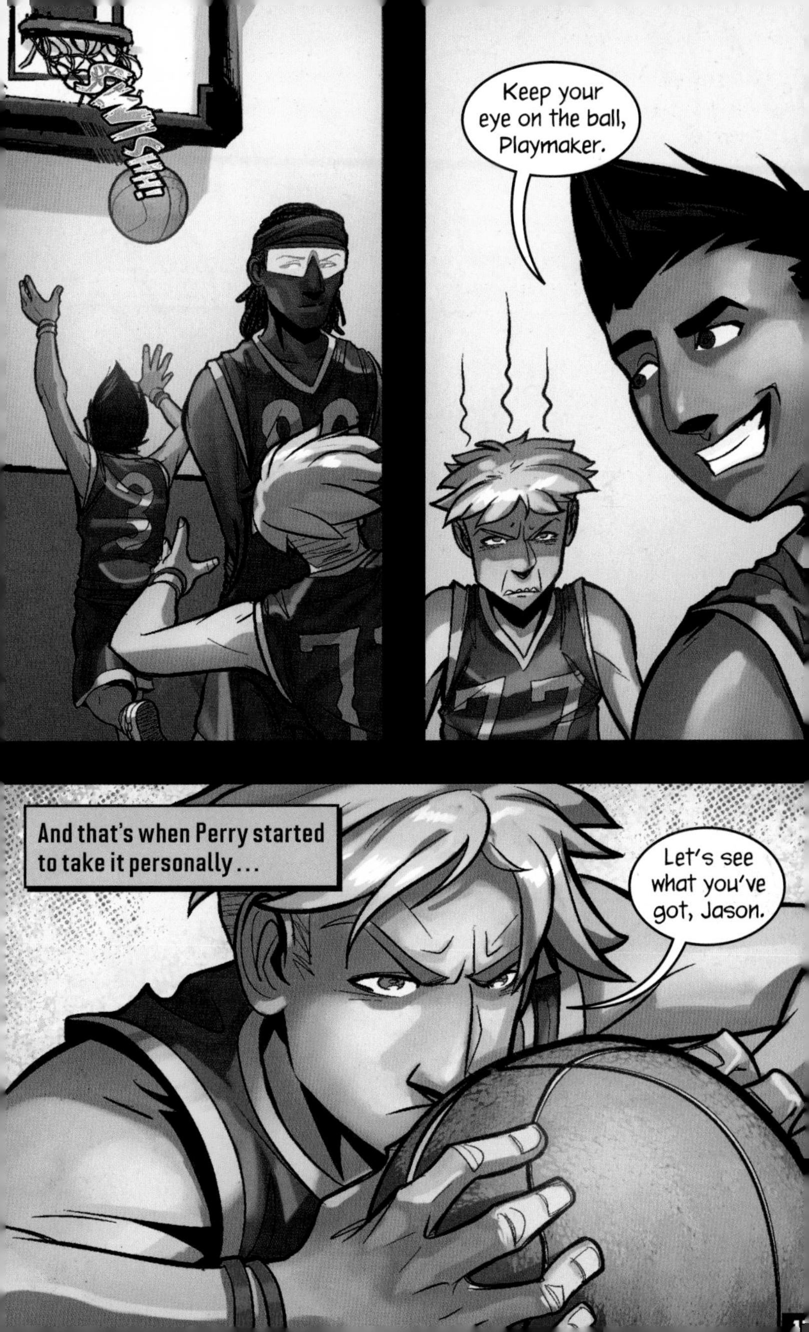
SWISHH!
Keep your eye on the ball, Playmaker.
And that's when Perry started to take it personally . . .
Let's see what you've got, Jason.

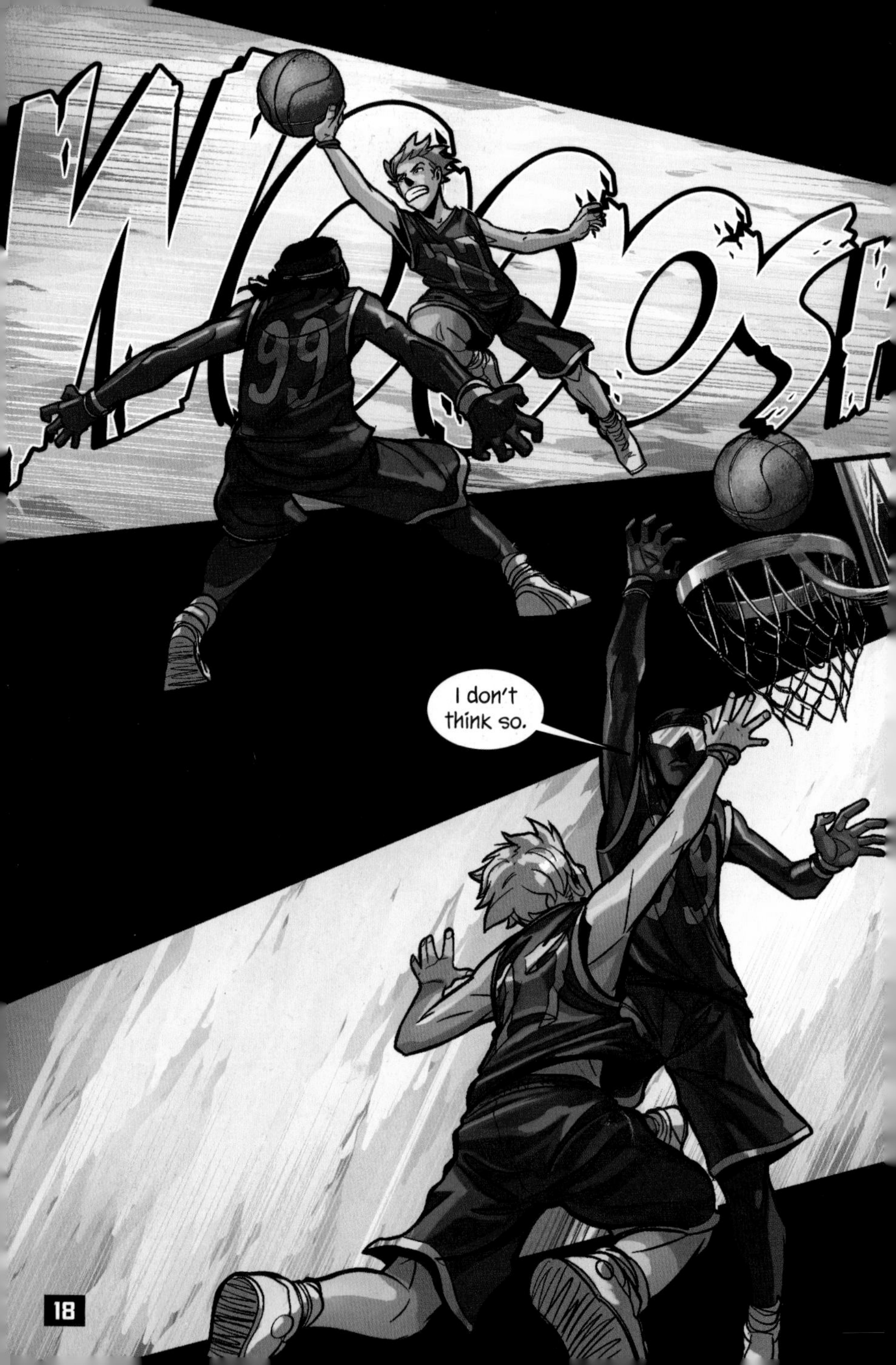
WOOOSH
I don't think so.

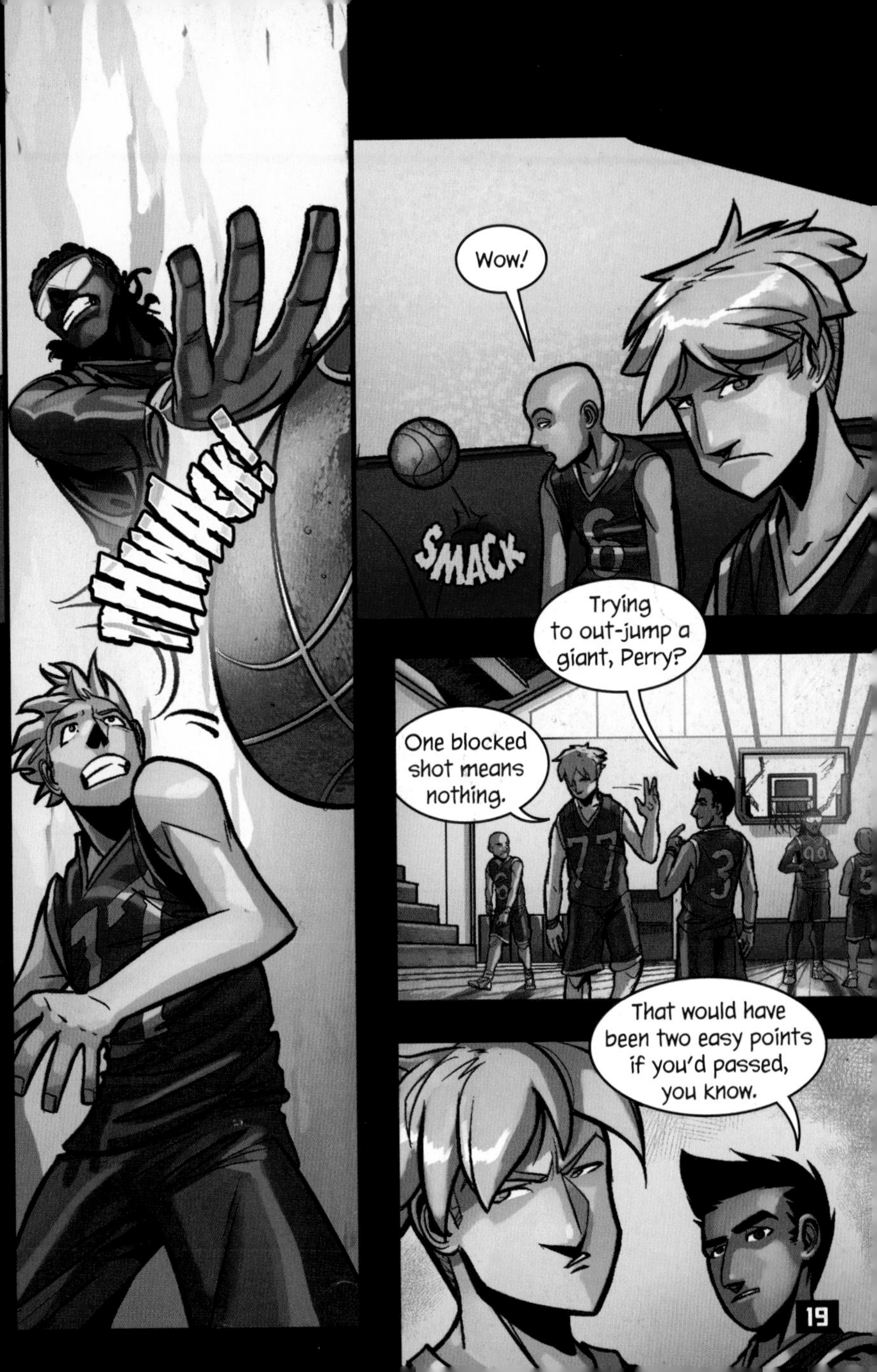
THWACK!
Wow!
SMACK
Trying to out-jump a giant, Perry?
One blocked shot means nothing.
That would have been two easy points if you'd passed, you know.

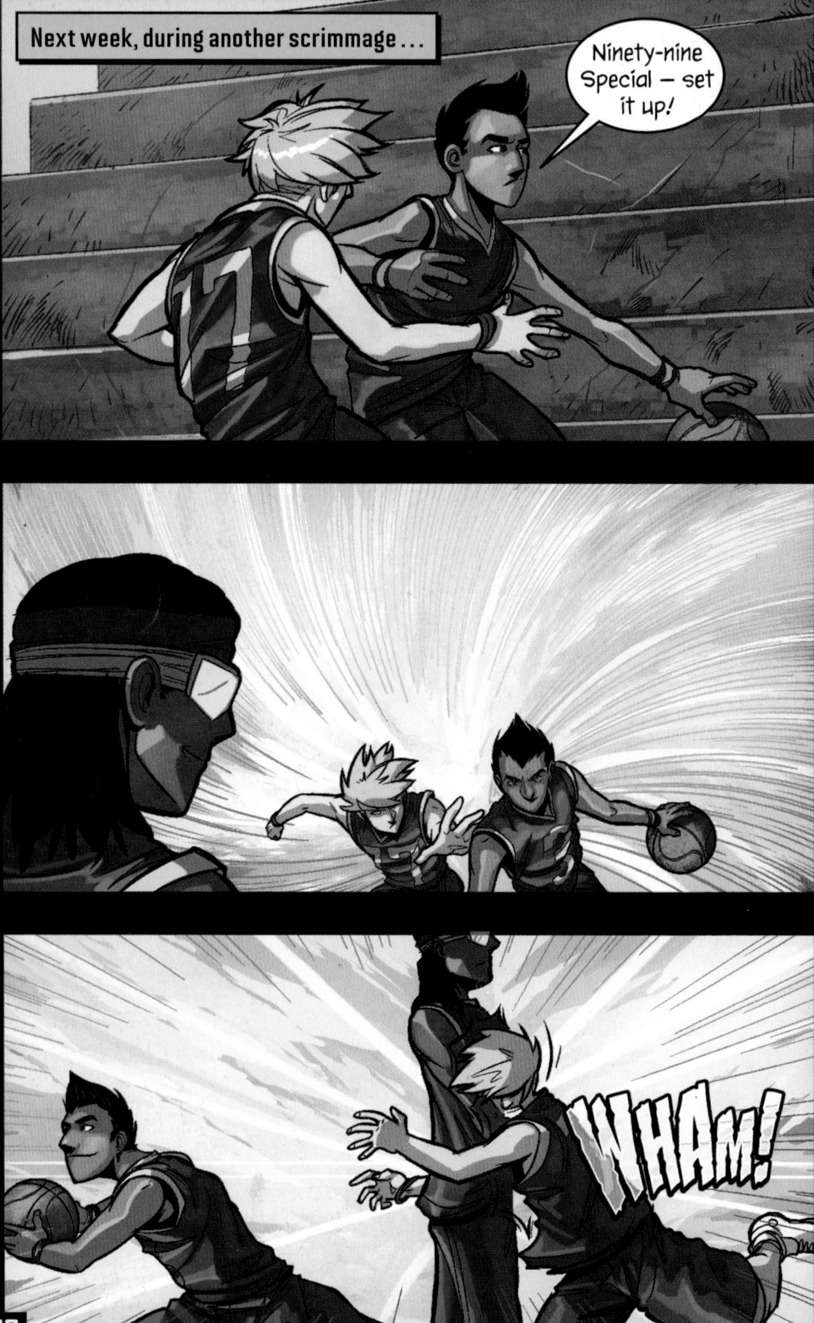
Next week, during another scrimmage . . .
Ninety-nine Special — set it up!
WHAM!

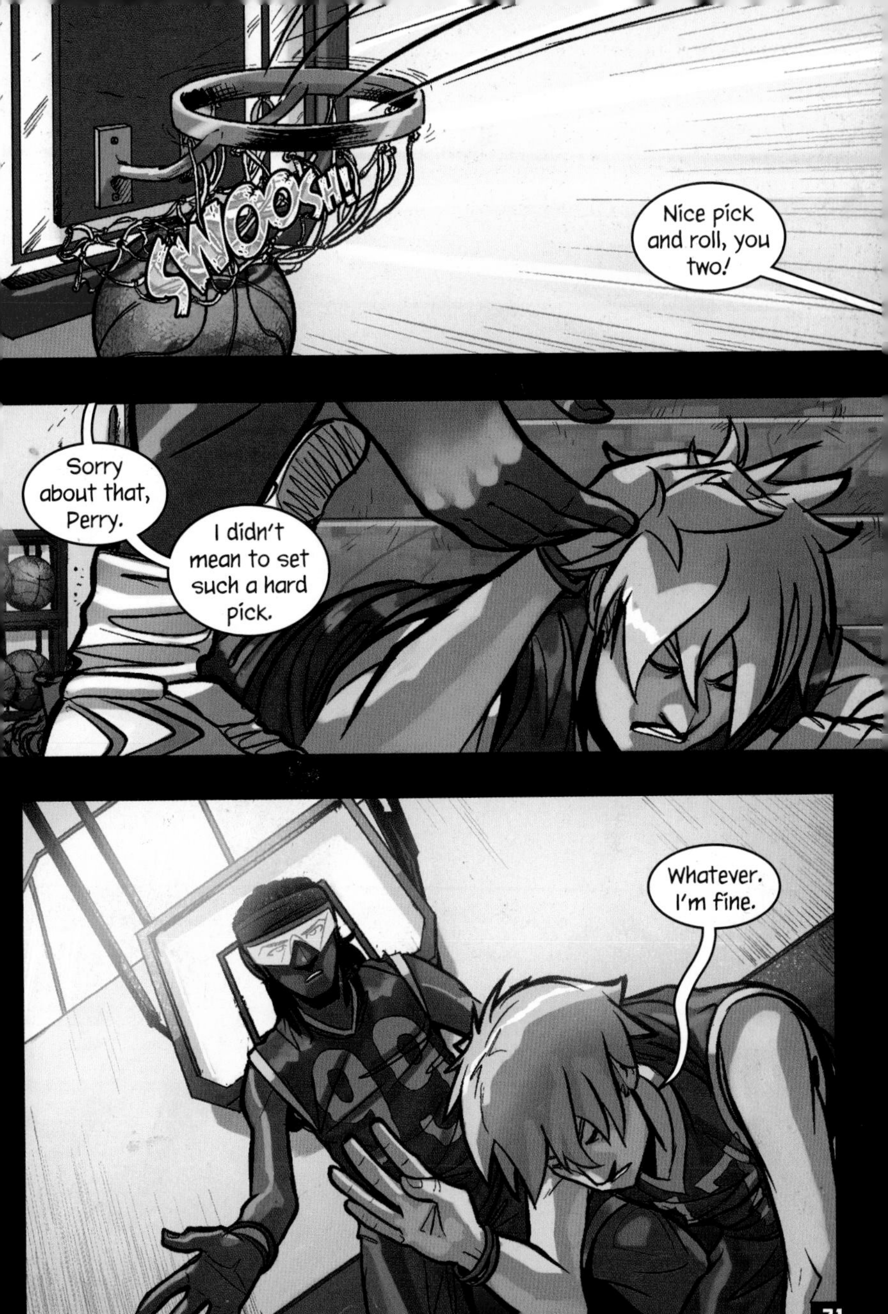
SWOOSH!
Nice pick and roll, you two!
Sorry about that, Perry.
I didn't mean to set such a hard pick.
Whatever. I'm fine.

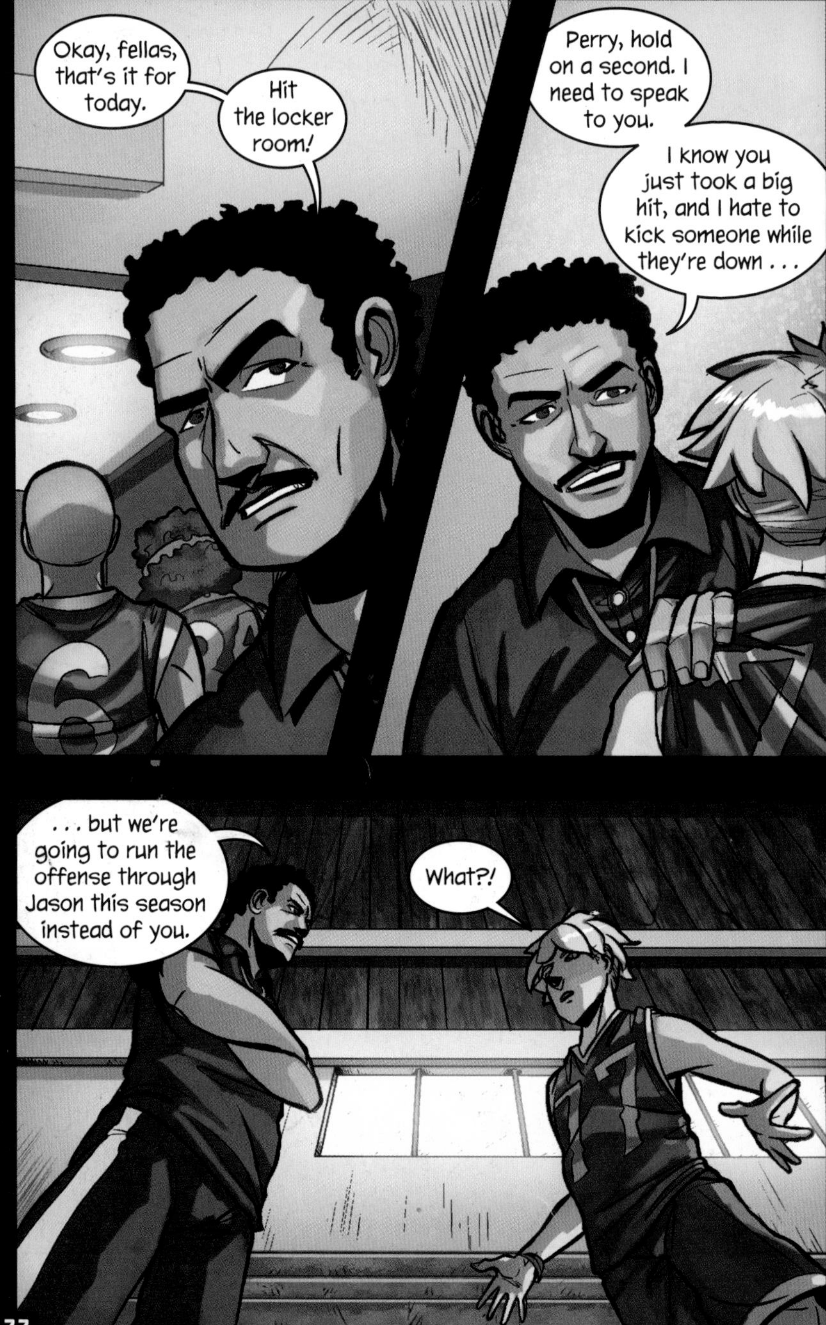
Okay, fellas, that's it for today.
Hit the locker room!
Perry, hold on a second. I need to speak to you.
I know you just took a big hit, and I hate to kick someone while they're down . . .
. . . but we're going to run the offense through Jason this season instead of you.
What?!

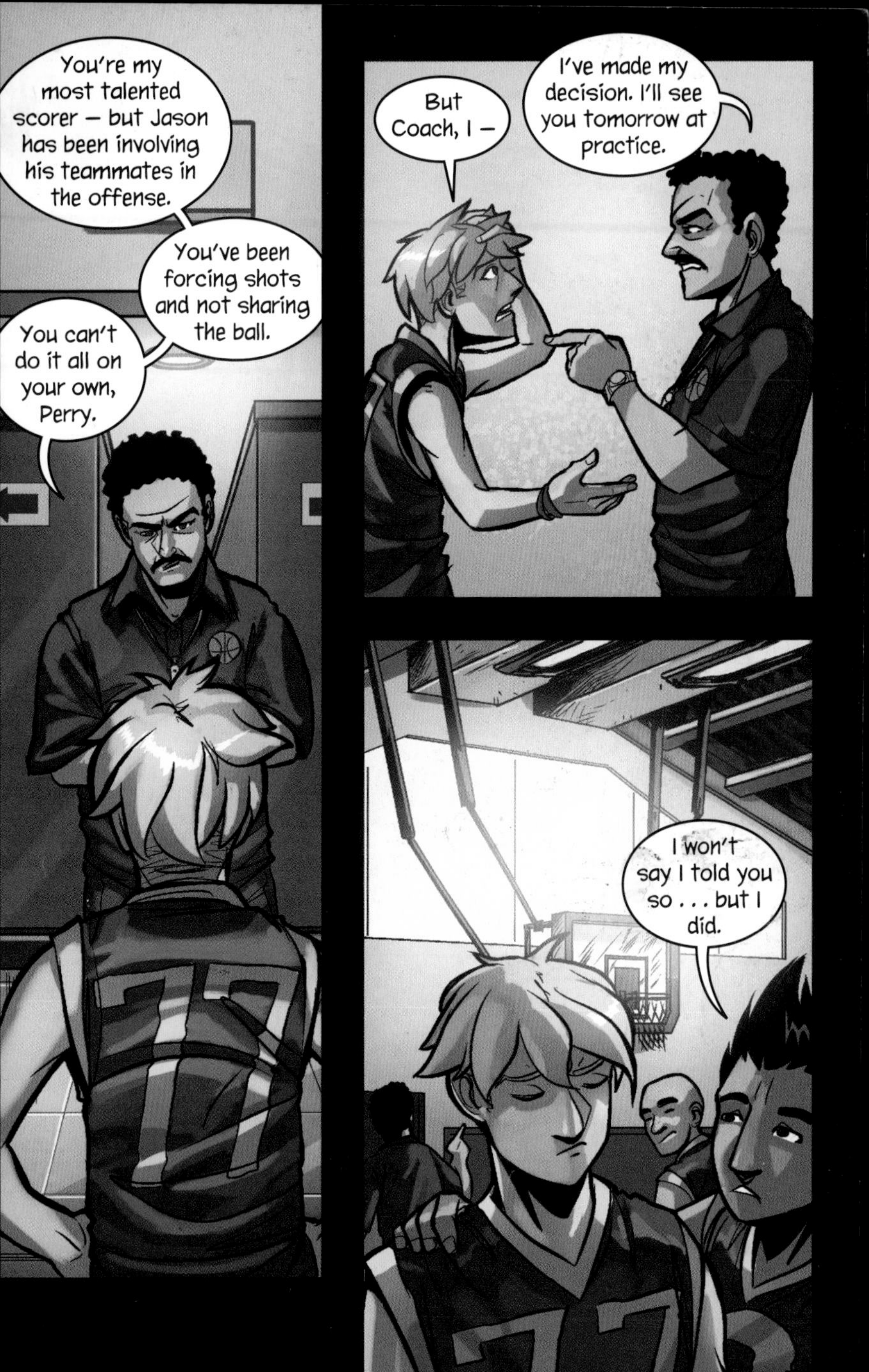
You're my most talented scorer — but Jason has been involving his teammates in the offense.
You've been forcing shots and not sharing the ball.
You can't do it all on your own, Perry.
But Coach, I —
I've made my decision. I'll see you tomorrow at practice.
I won't say I told you so . . . but I did.

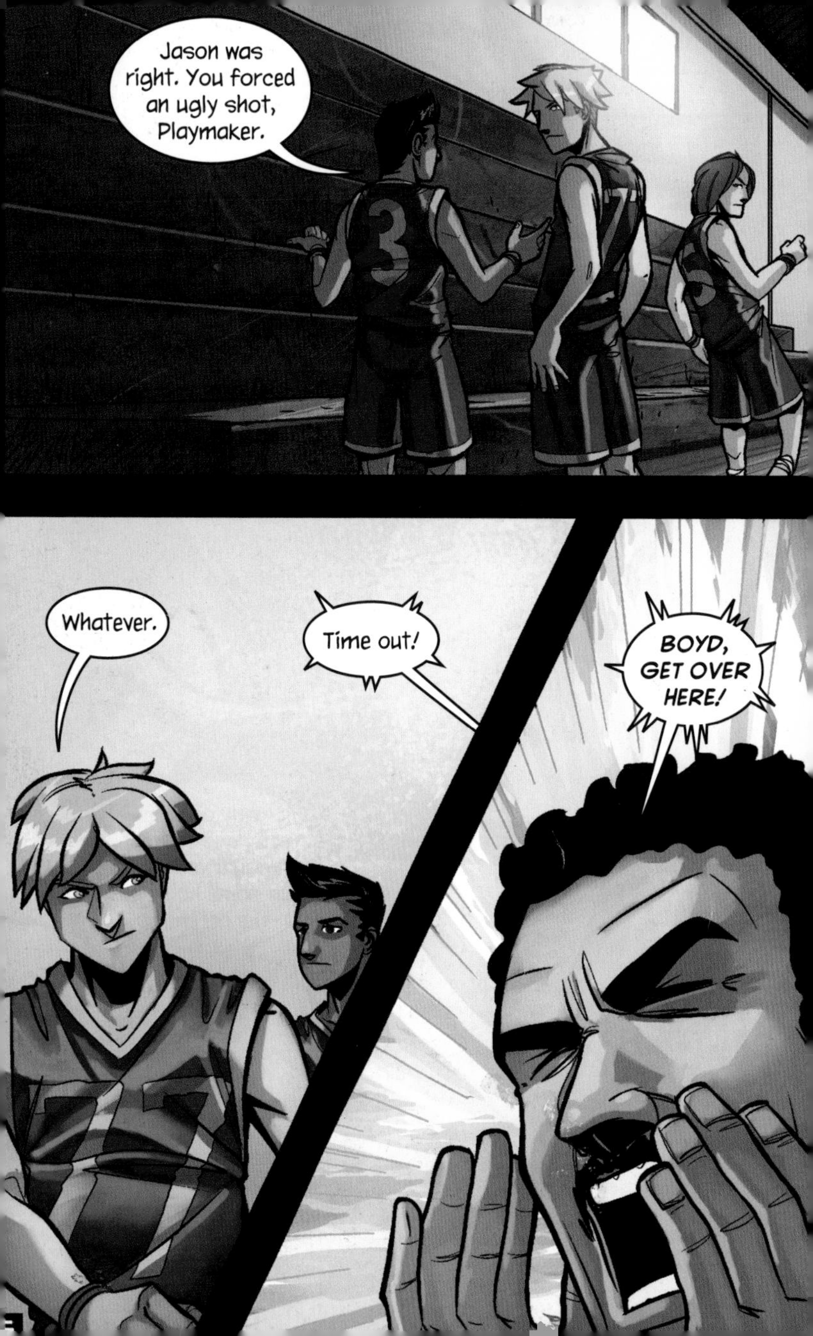
Jason was right. You forced an ugly shot, Playmaker.
Whatever.
Time out!
BOYD, GET OVER HERE!

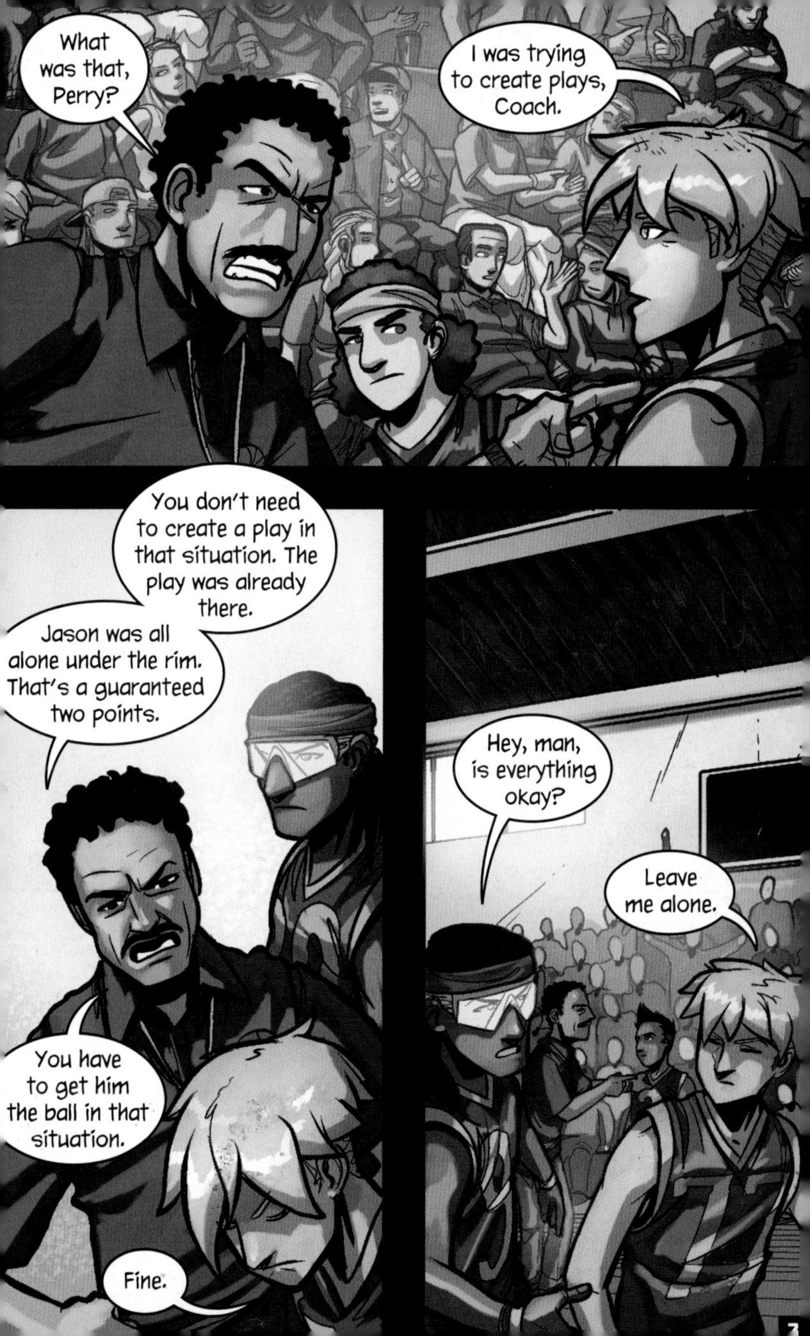
What was that, Perry?
I was trying to create plays, Coach.
You don't need to create a play in that situation. The play was already there.
Jason was all alone under the rim. That's a guaranteed two points.
You have to get him the ball in that situation.
Fine.
Hey, man, is everything okay?
Leave me alone.

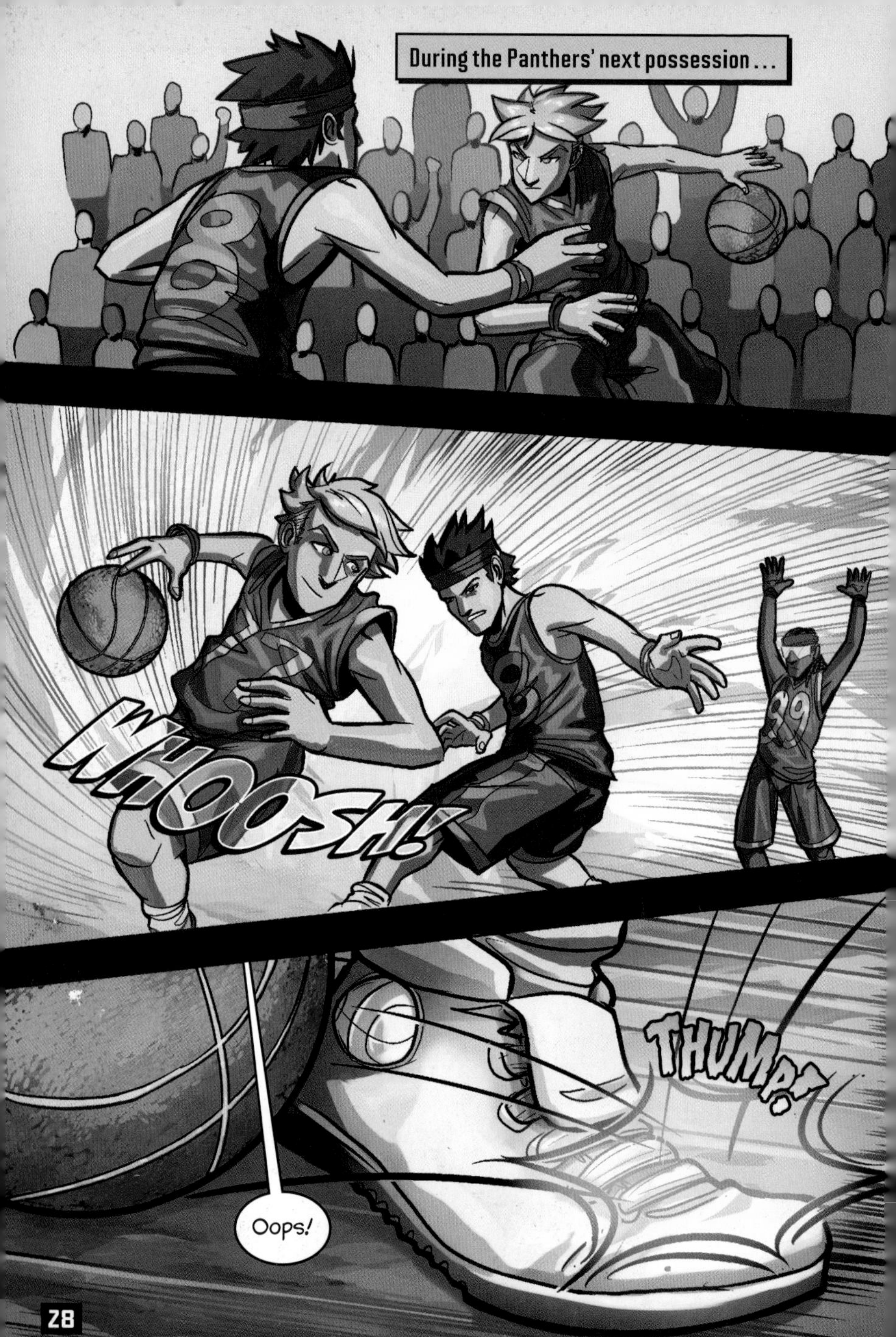
During the Panthers' next possession . . .
WHOOSH!
THUMP!
Oops!

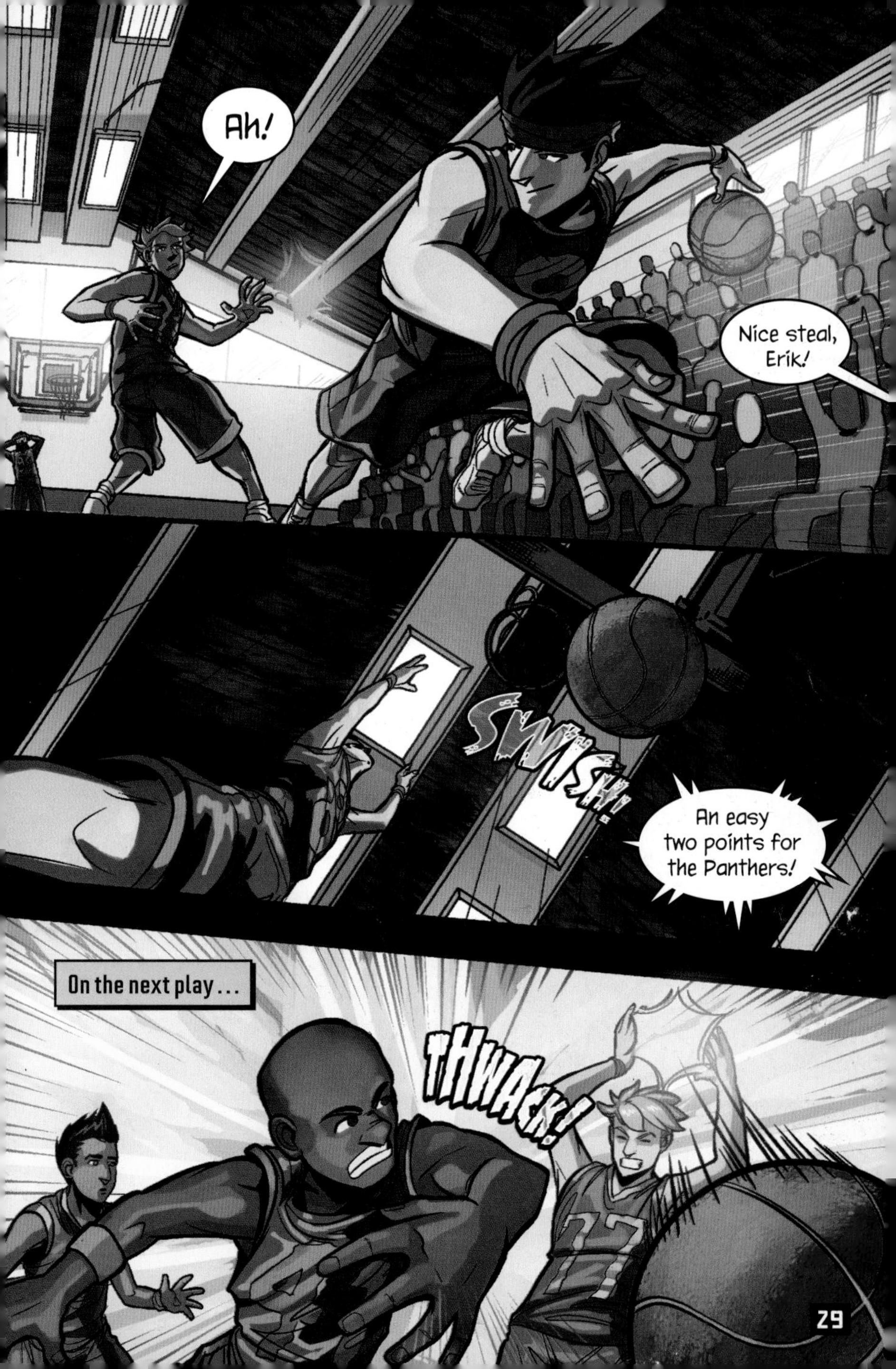
Ah!
Nice steal, Erik!
SWISH!
An easy two points for the Panthers!
On the next play . . .
THWACK!

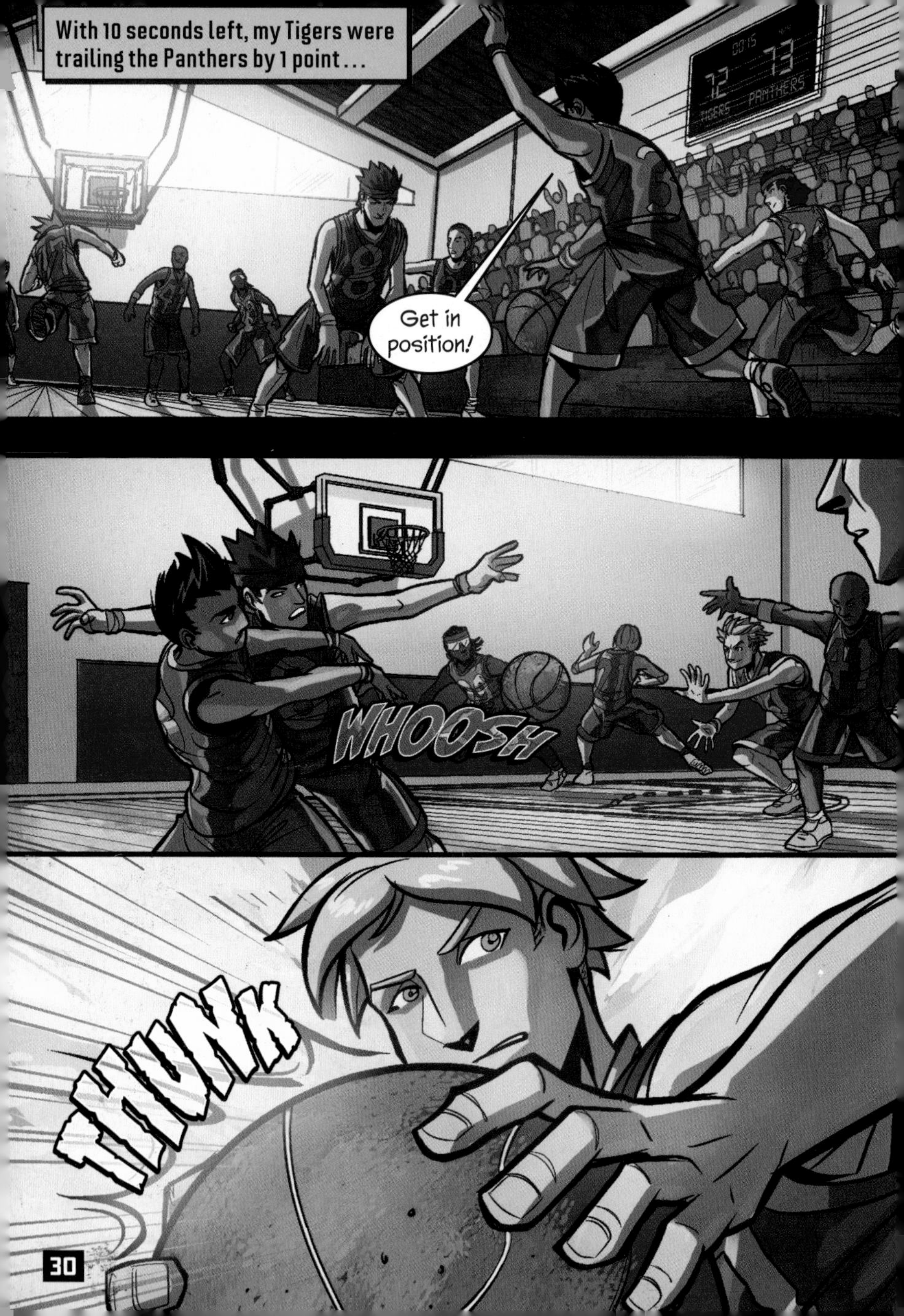
With 10 seconds left, my Tigers were trailing the Panthers by 1 point . . .
TIGERS
PANTHERS
Get in position!
WHOOSH
THUNK

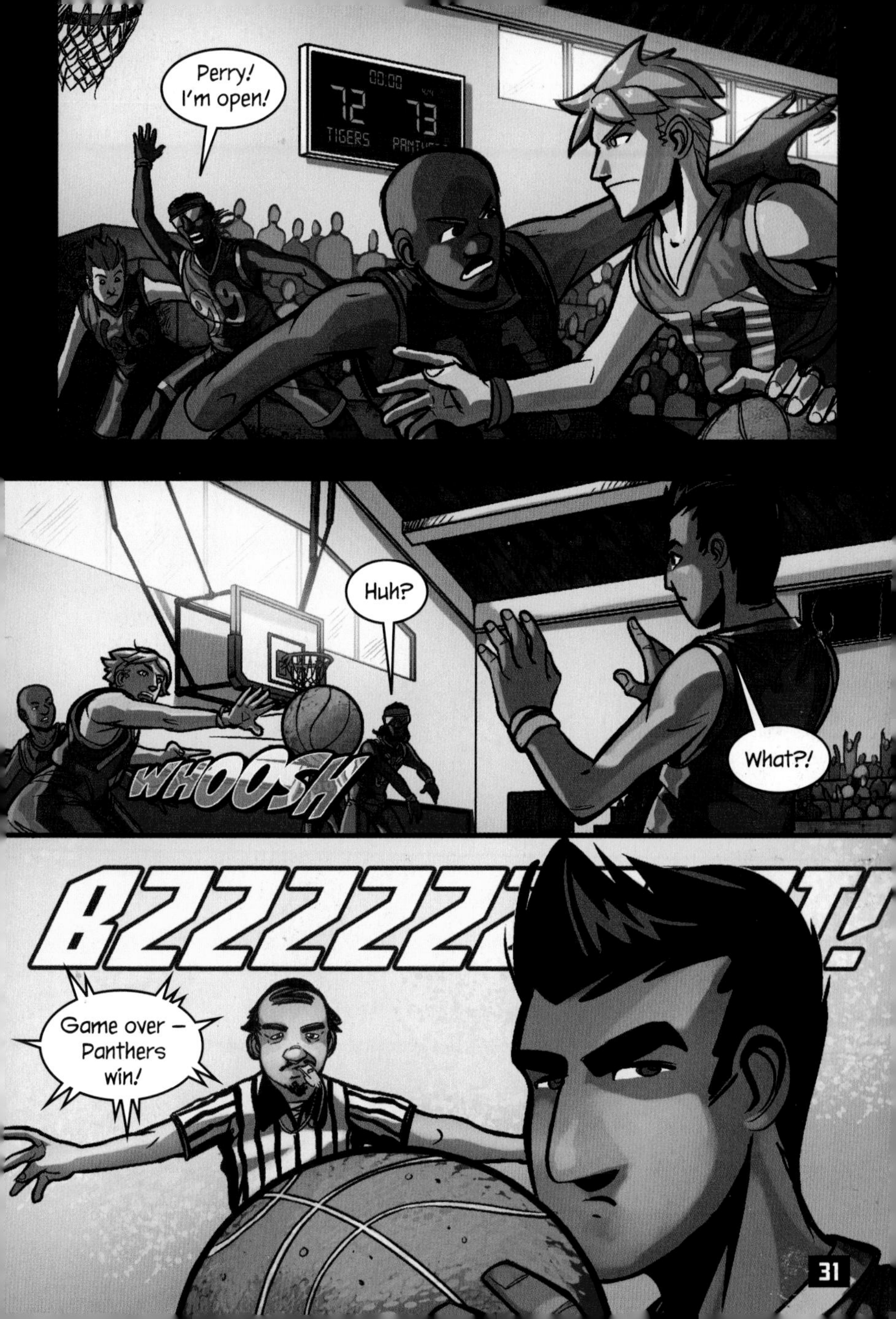
Perry! I'm open!
00:00
72 73
TIGERS
Huh?
WHOOSH
What?!
Game over – Panthers win!

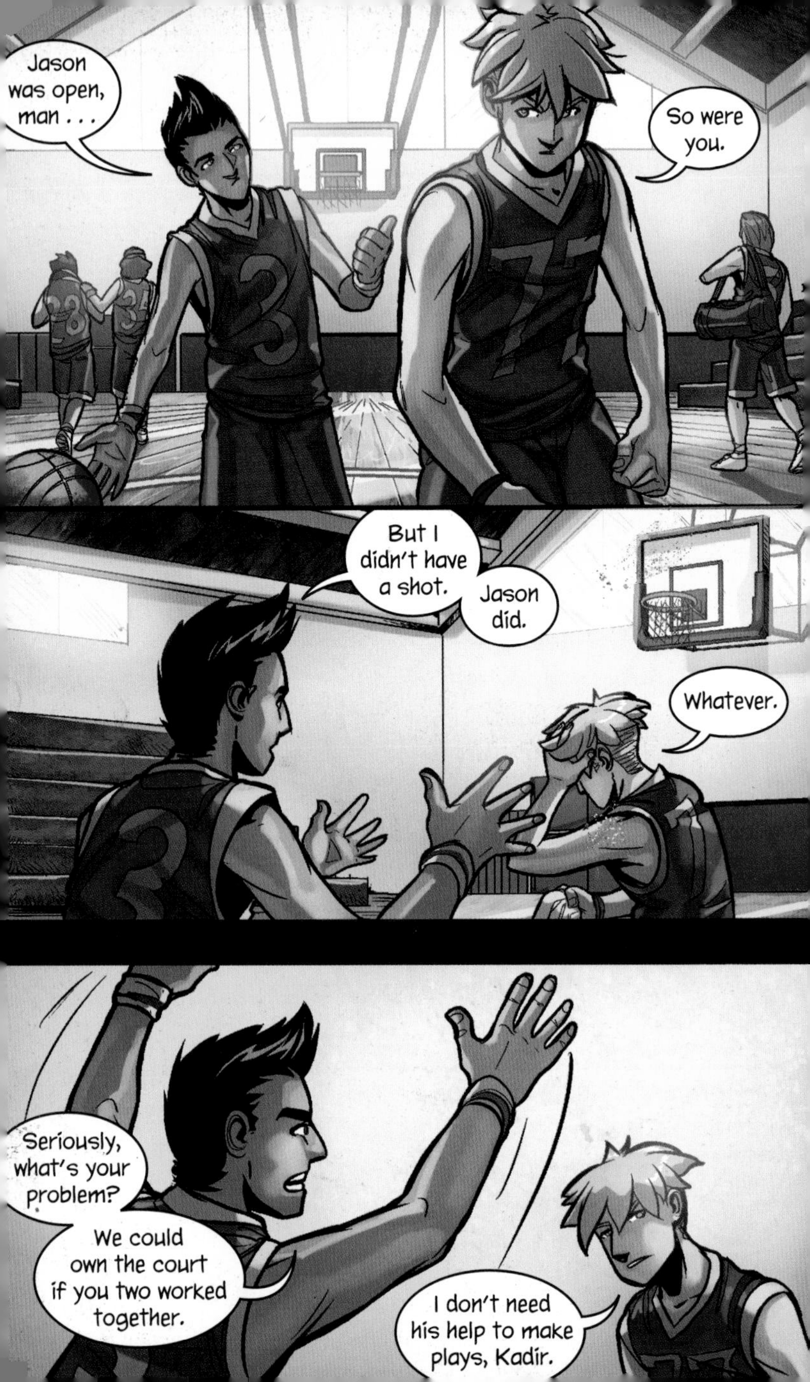
Jason was open, man . . .
So were you.
But I didn't have a shot.
Jason did.
Whatever.
Seriously, what's your problem?
We could own the court if you two worked together.
I don't need his help to make plays, Kadir.

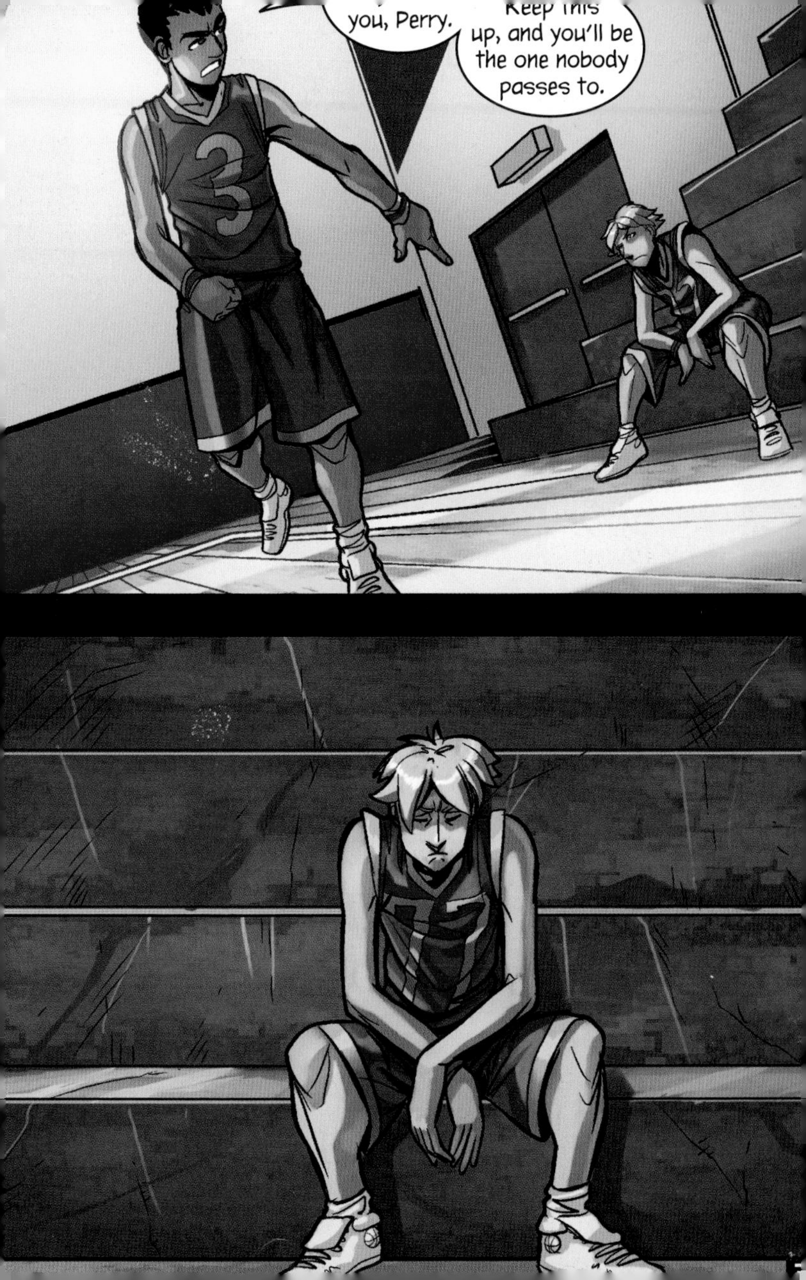
you, Perry.
Keep this up, and you'll be the one nobody passes to.

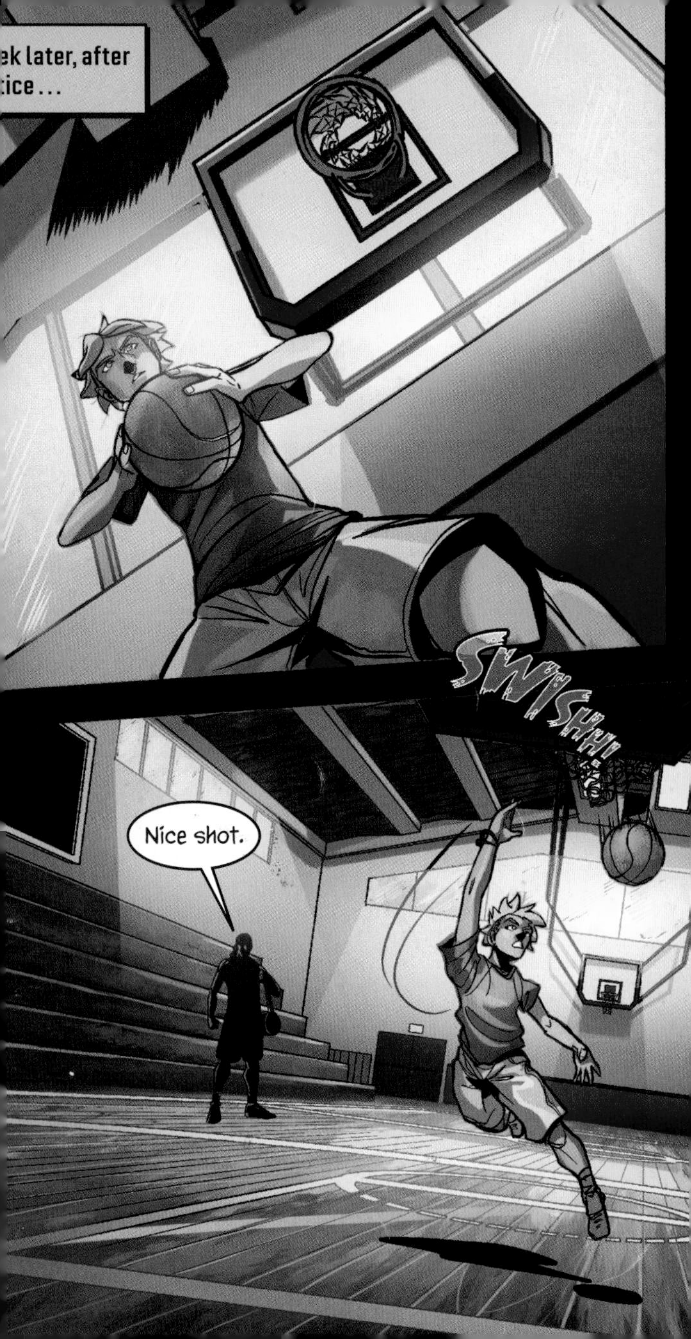
ek later, after
tice...
SWISH!
Nice shot.

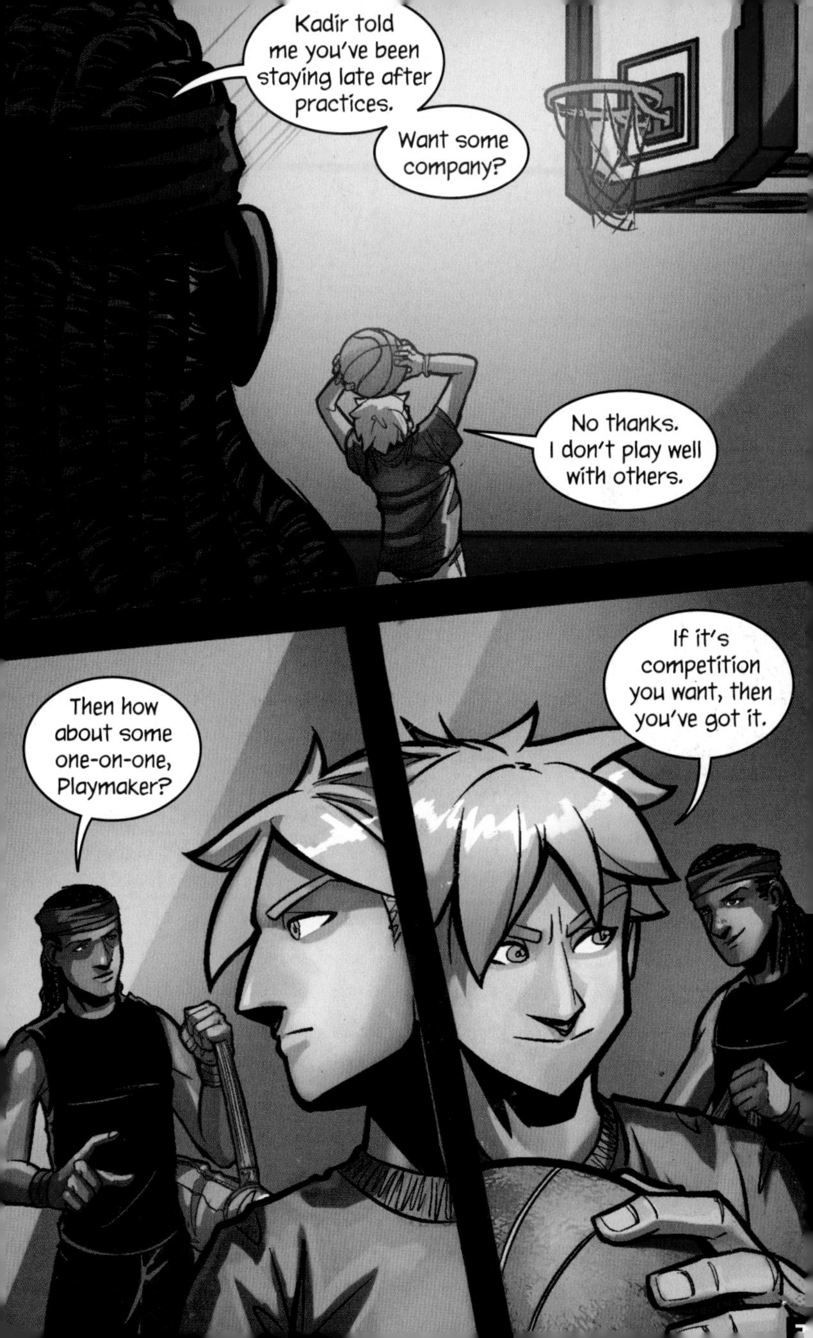
Kadir told me you've been staying late after practices.
Want some company?
No thanks. I don't play well with others.
Then how about some one-on-one, Playmaker?
If it's competition you want, then you've got it.

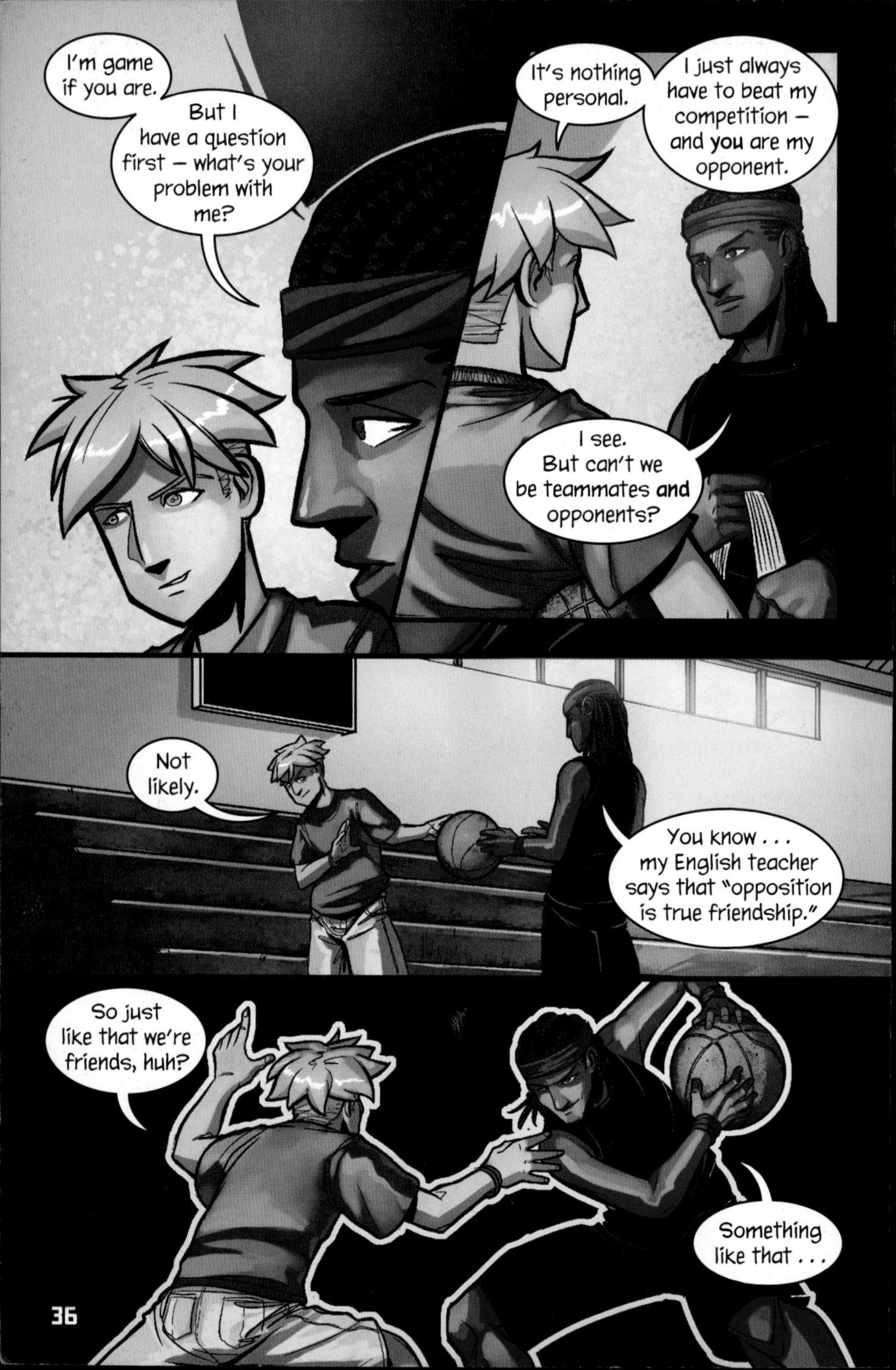

I'm game if you are.
But I have a question first – what's your problem with me?
It's nothing personal.
I just always have to beat my competition – and **you** are my opponent.
I see. But can't we be teammates **and** opponents?
Not likely.
You know . . . my English teacher says that "opposition is true friendship."
So just like that we're friends, huh?
Something like that . . .

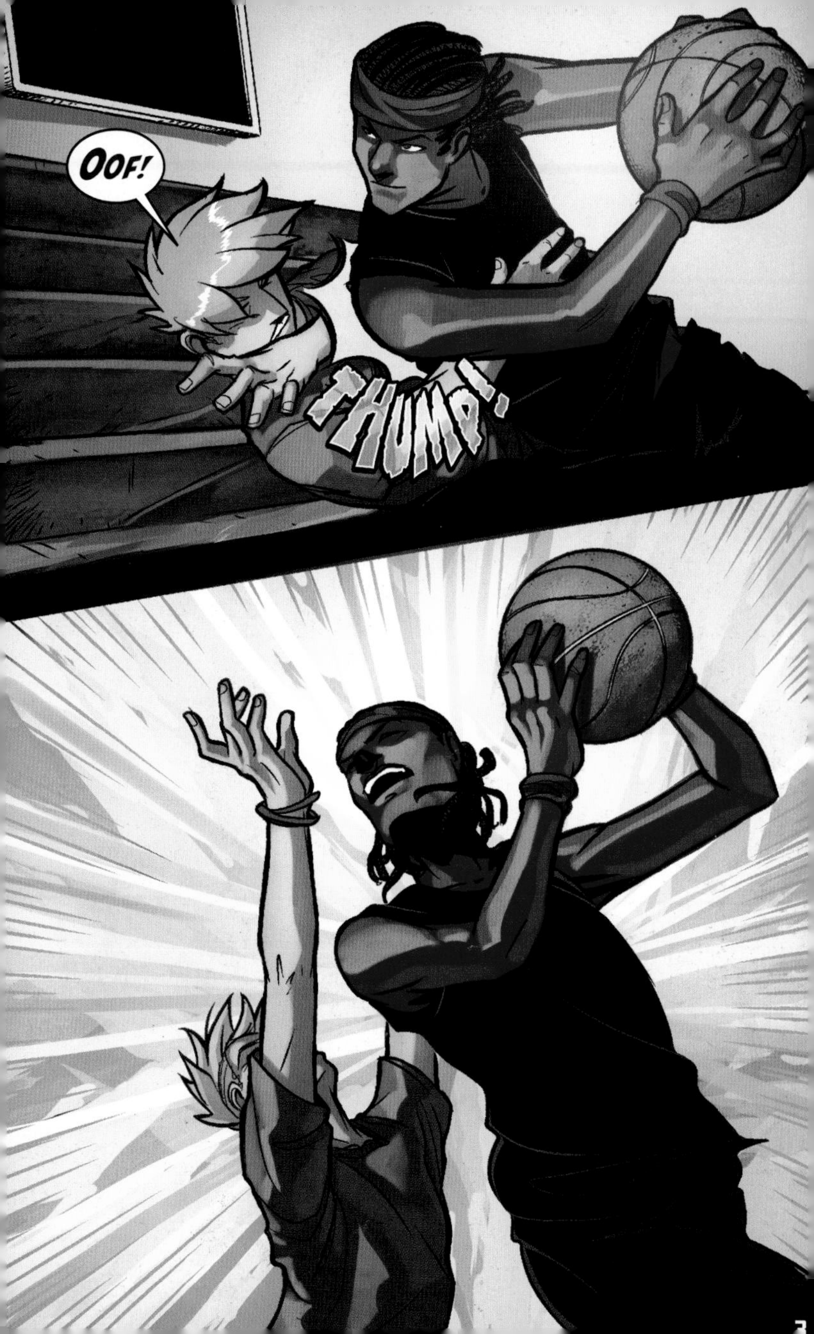
OOF!
THUMP!

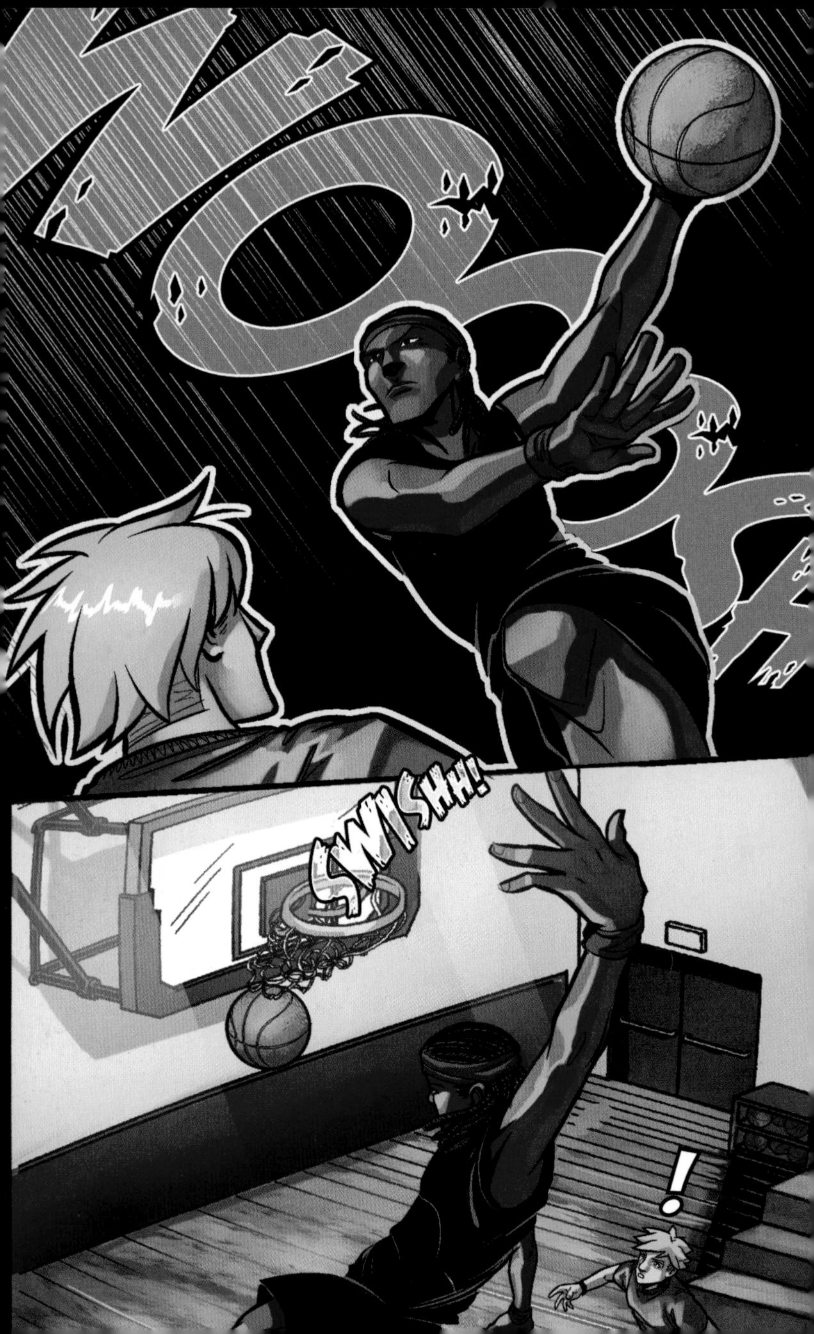
SWISHH!
!

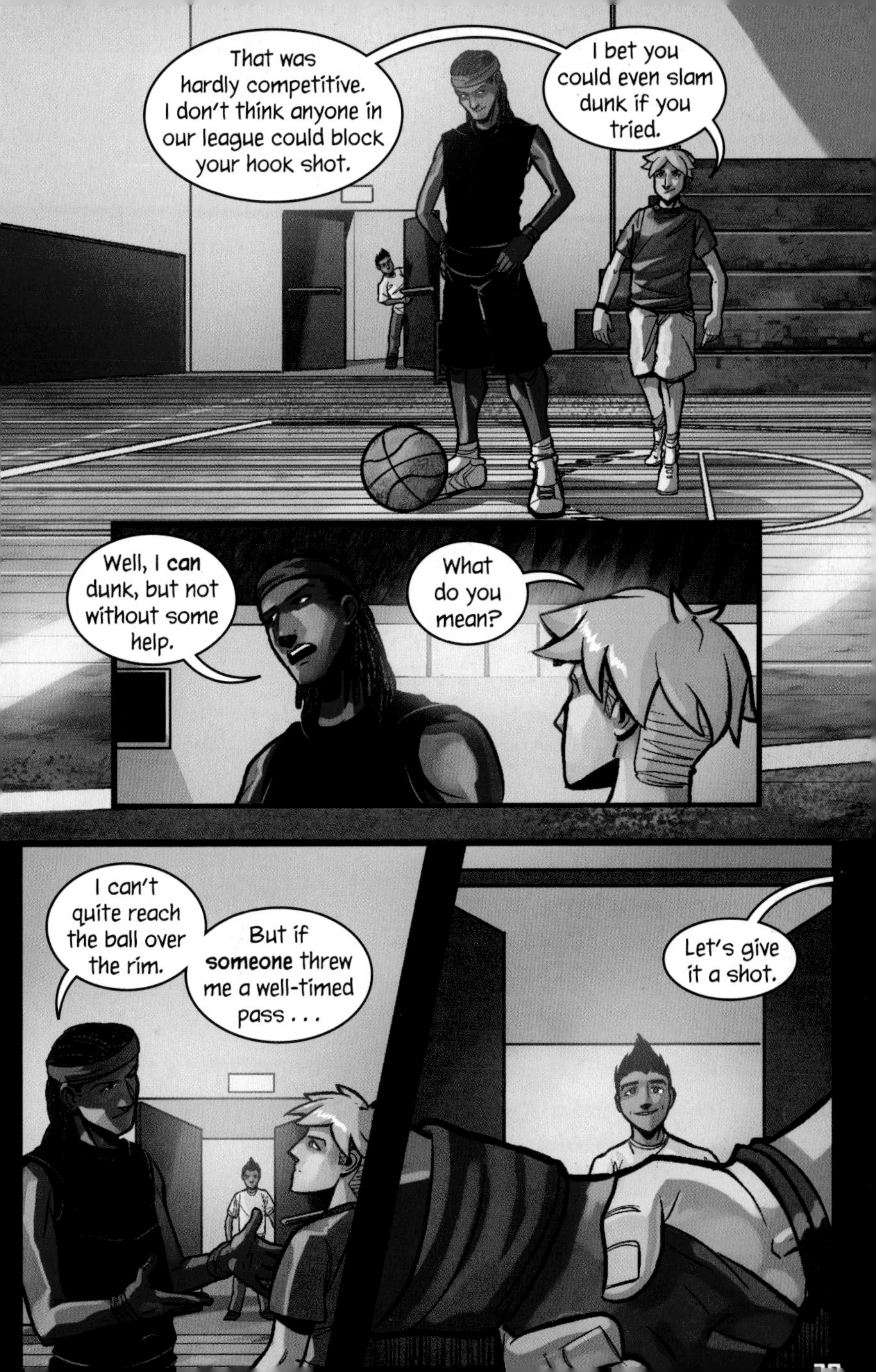
That was hardly competitive. I don't think anyone in our league could block your hook shot.
I bet you could even slam dunk if you tried.
Well, I **can** dunk, but not without some help.
What do you mean?
I can't quite reach the ball over the rim.
But if **someone** threw me a well-timed pass . . .
Let's give it a shot.

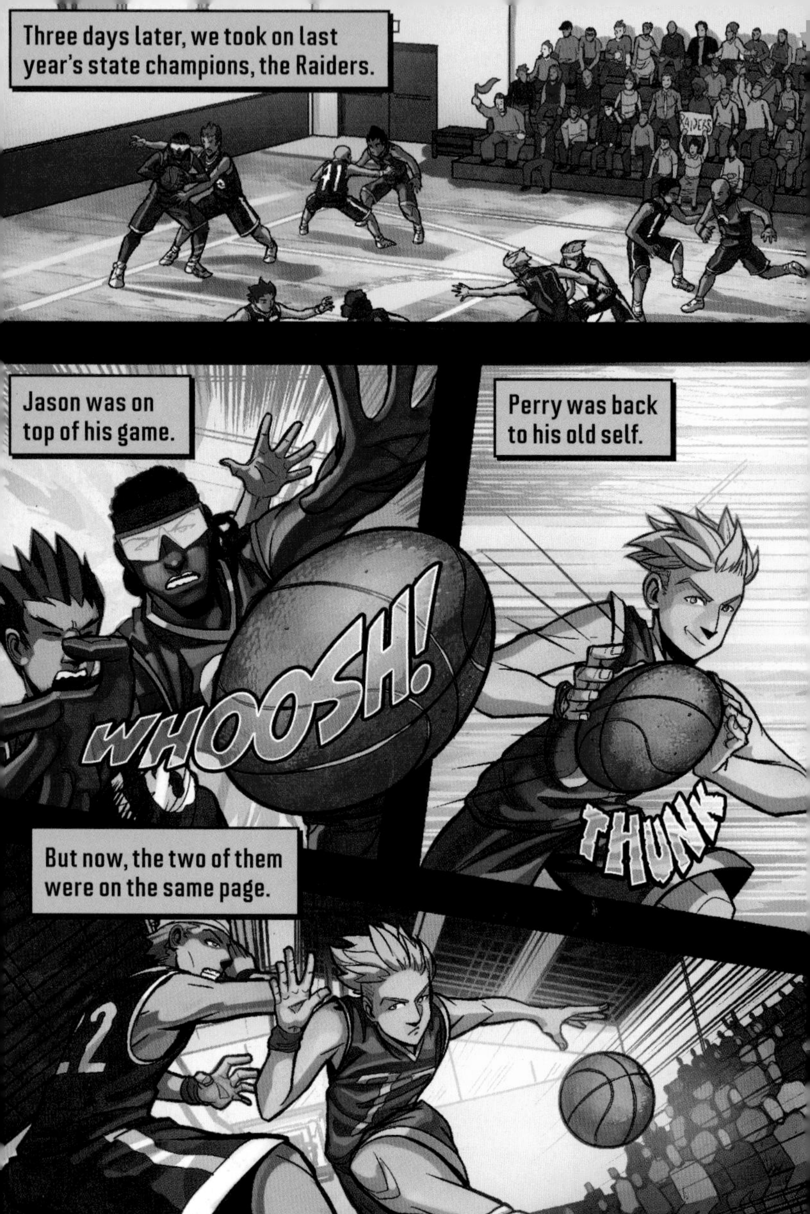

Three days later, we took on last year's state champions, the Raiders.
Jason was on top of his game.
WHOOSH!
Perry was back to his old self.
But now, the two of them were on the same page.

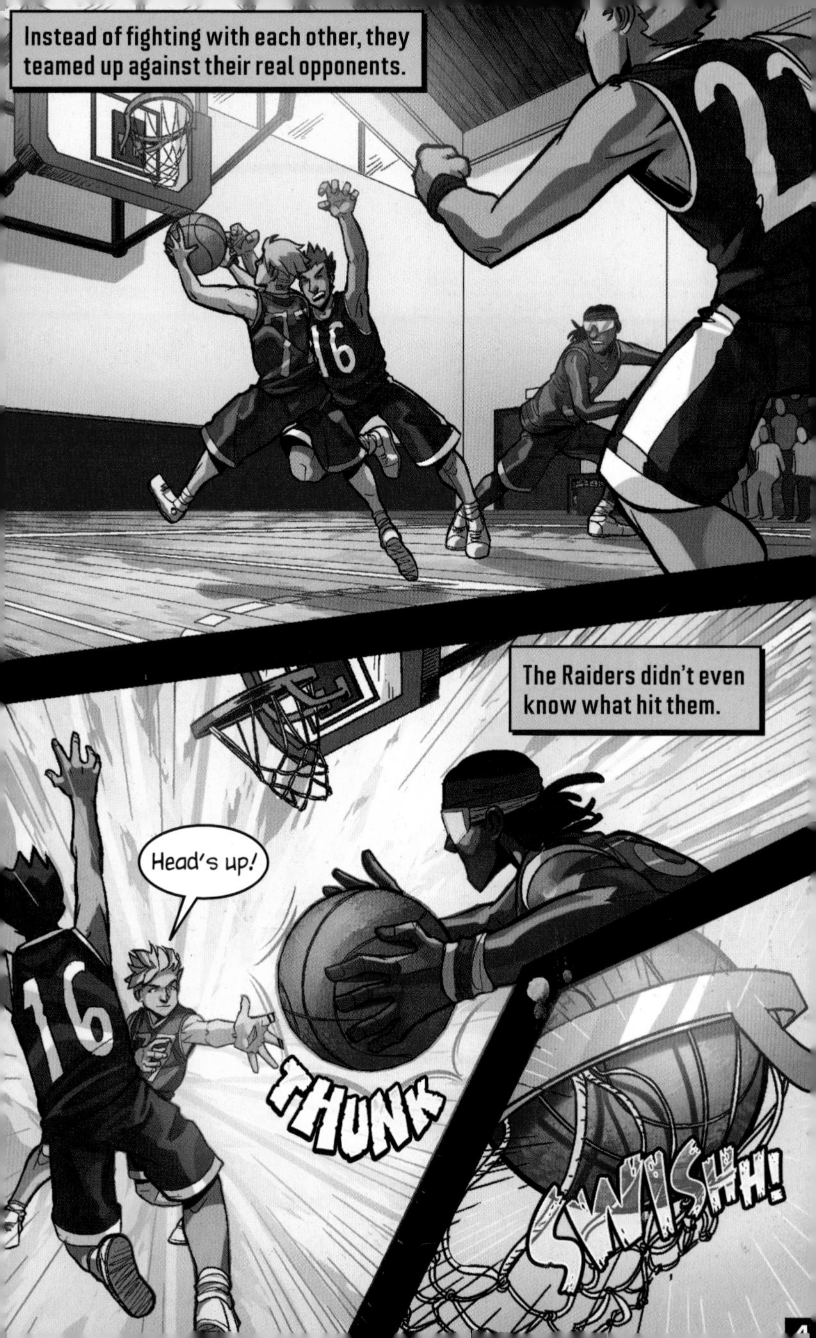
Instead of fighting with each other, they teamed up against their real opponents.
The Raiders didn't even know what hit them.
Head's up!
THUNK
SWISHH!

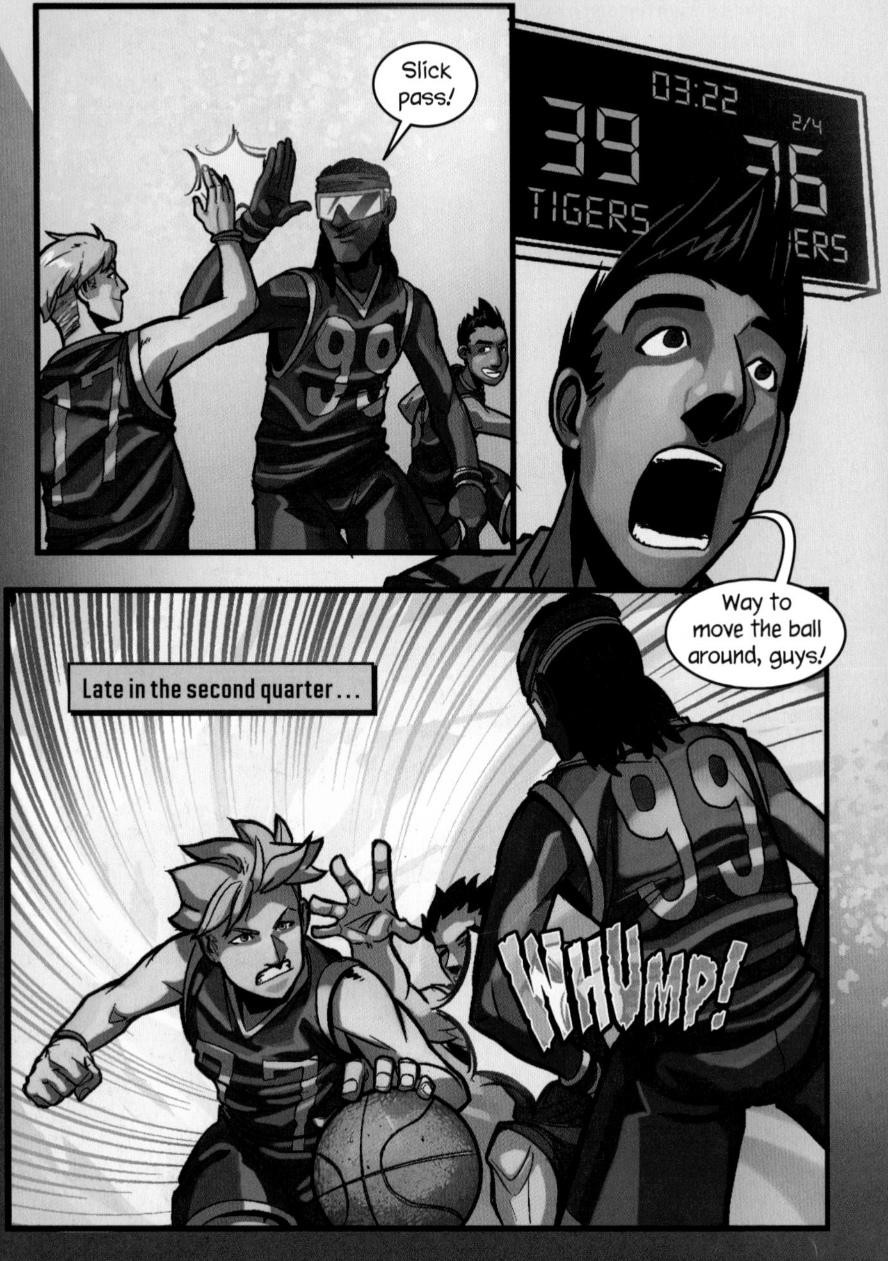
Slick pass!
03:22
39
TIGERS
2/4
Way to move the ball around, guys!
Late in the second quarter . . .
WHUMP!

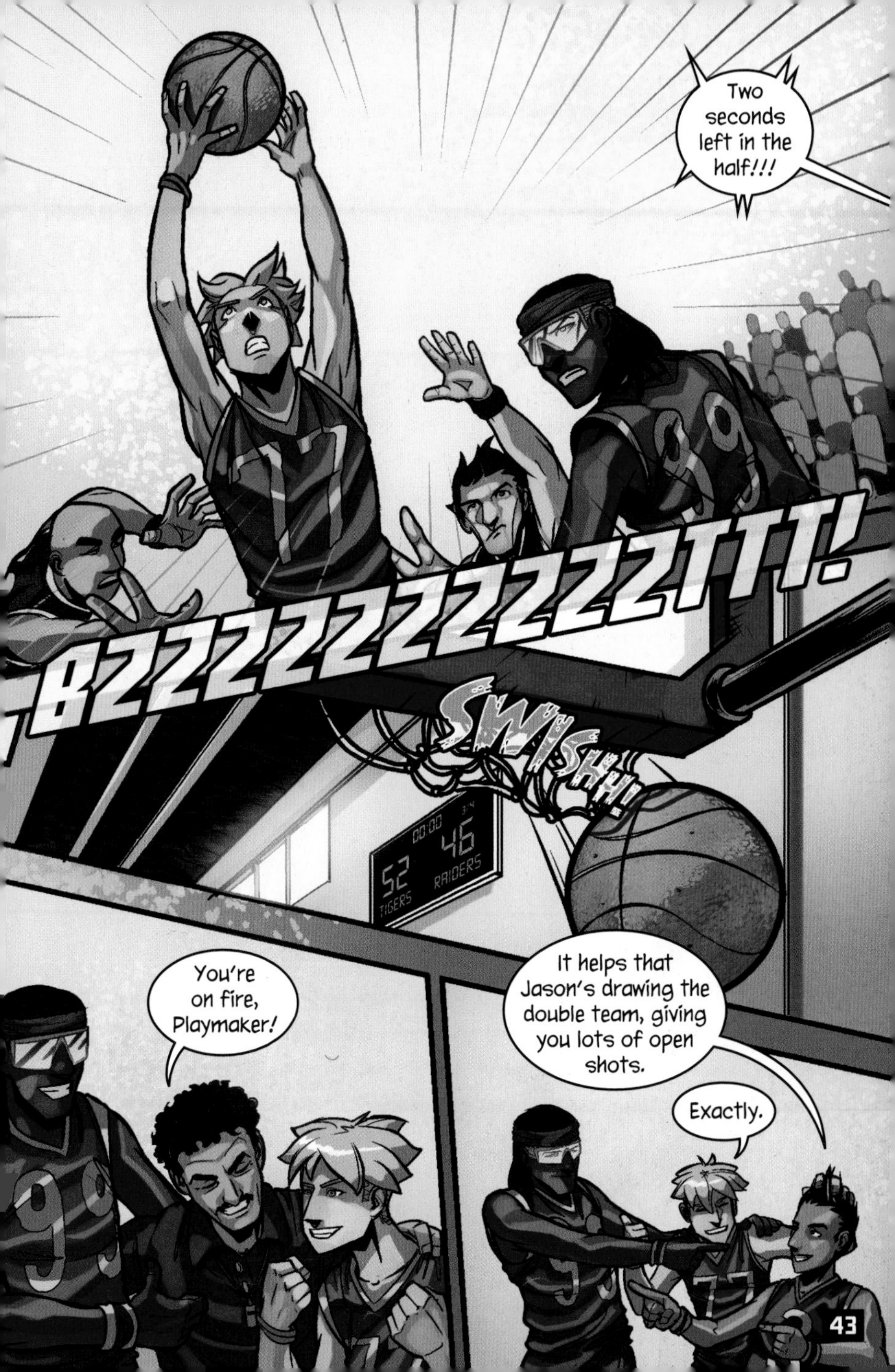
Two seconds left in the half!!!
BZZZZZZZZZZZTTT!
SWISH!
00:00
52
TIGERS
46
RAIDERS
You're on fire, Playmaker!
It helps that Jason's drawing the double team, giving you lots of open shots.
Exactly.

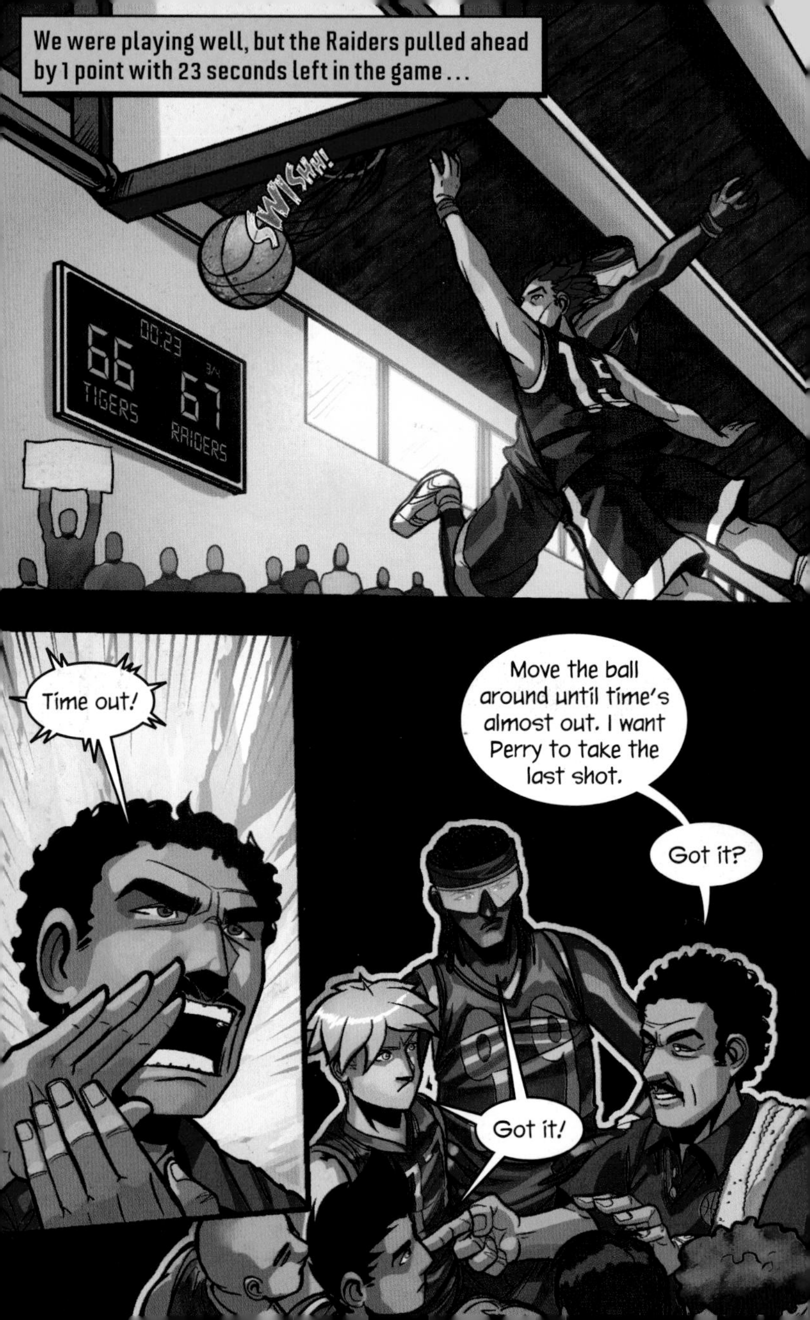

We were playing well, but the Raiders pulled ahead by 1 point with 23 seconds left in the game . . .
SWISHH!
00:23
66
TIGERS
67
RAIDERS
Time out!
Move the ball around until time's almost out. I want Perry to take the last shot.
Got it?
Got it!

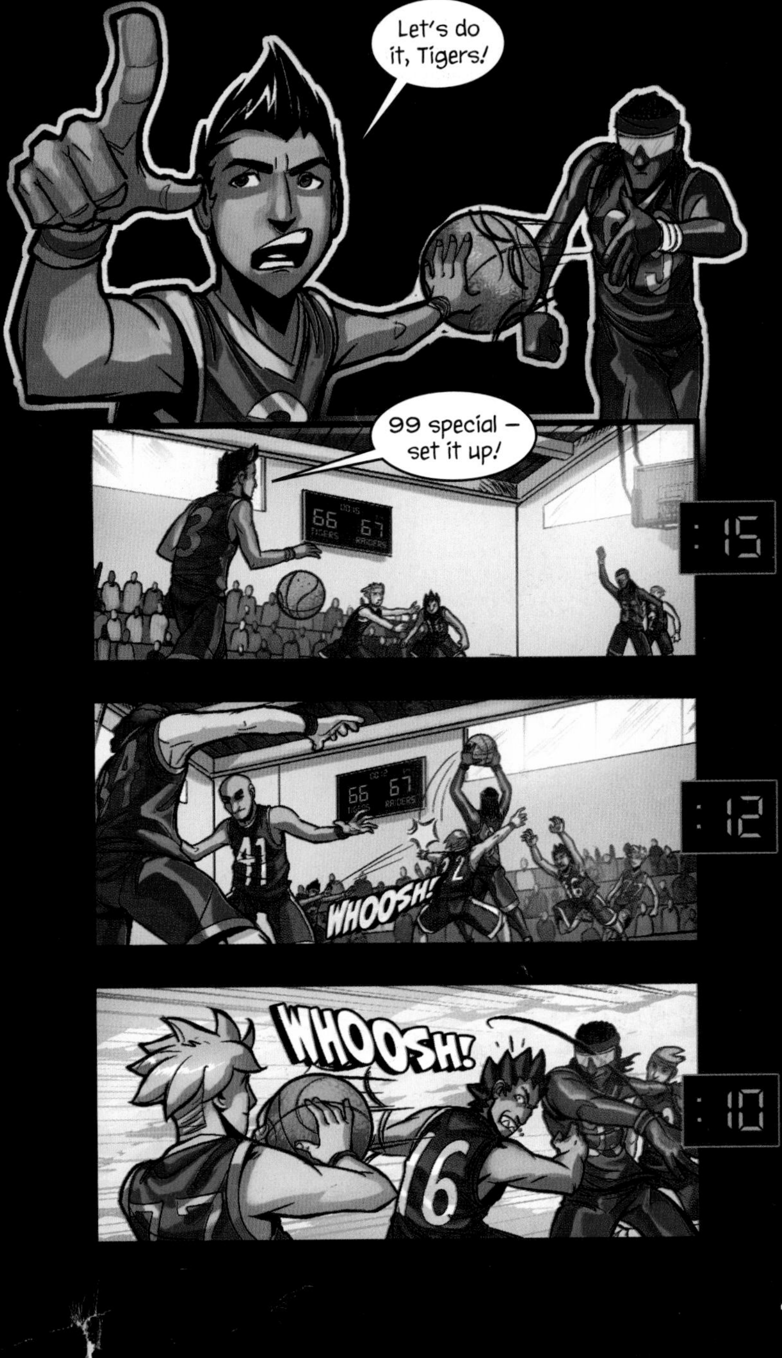

Let's do it, Tigers!
99 special — set it up!
:15
:12
WHOOSH!
WHOOSH!
:10

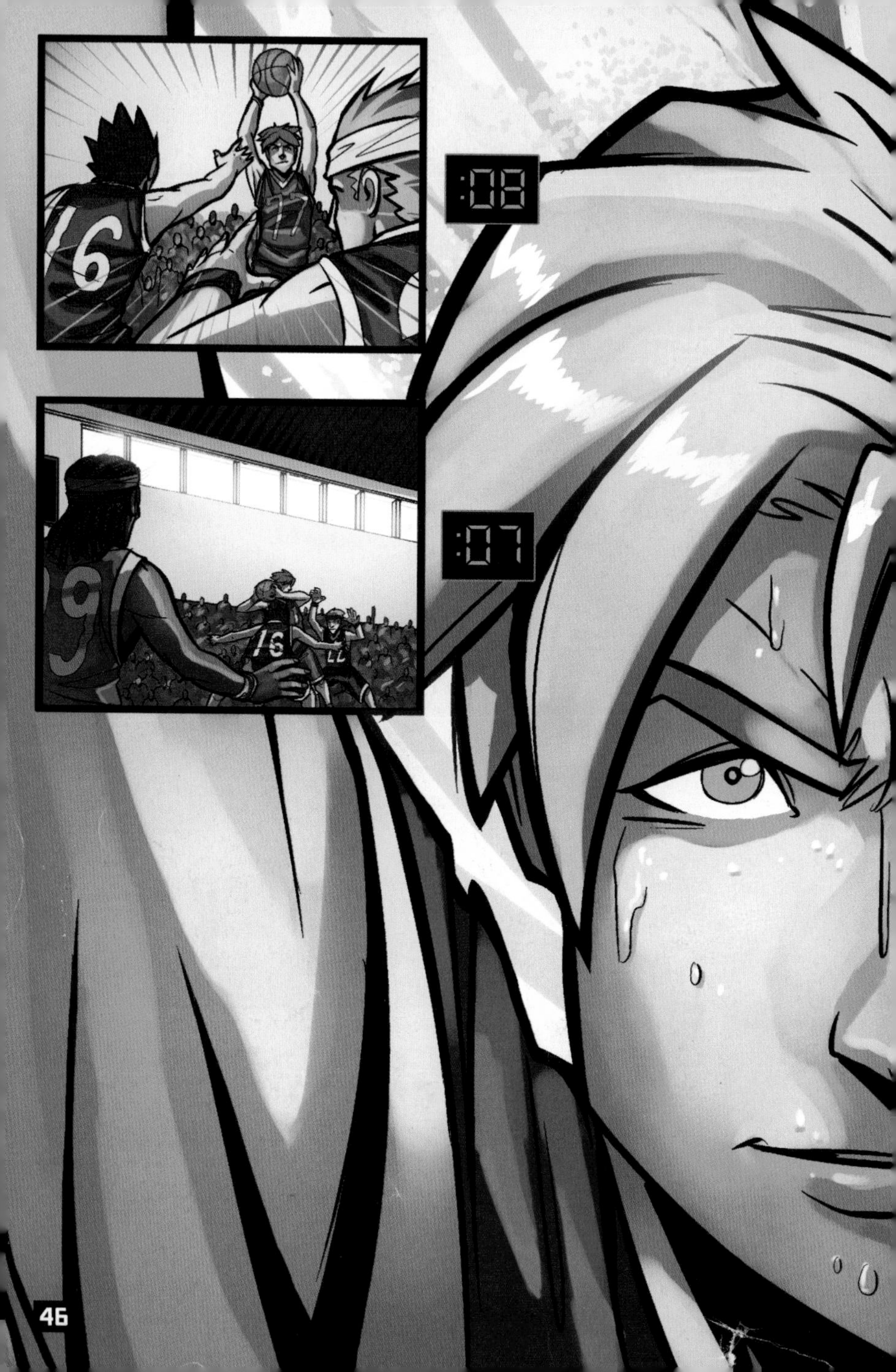
:08
:07

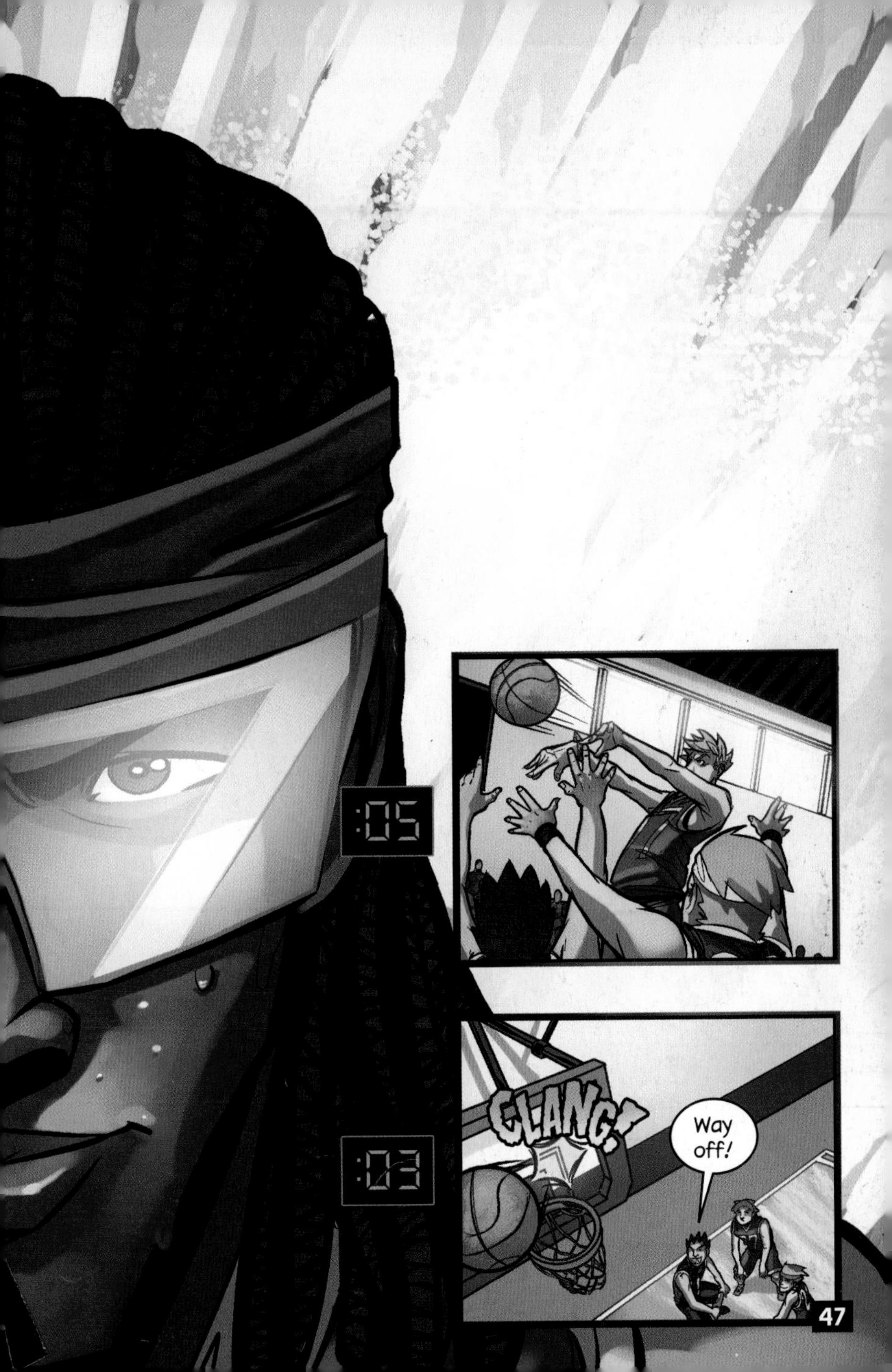
:05
:03
CLANG!
Way off!

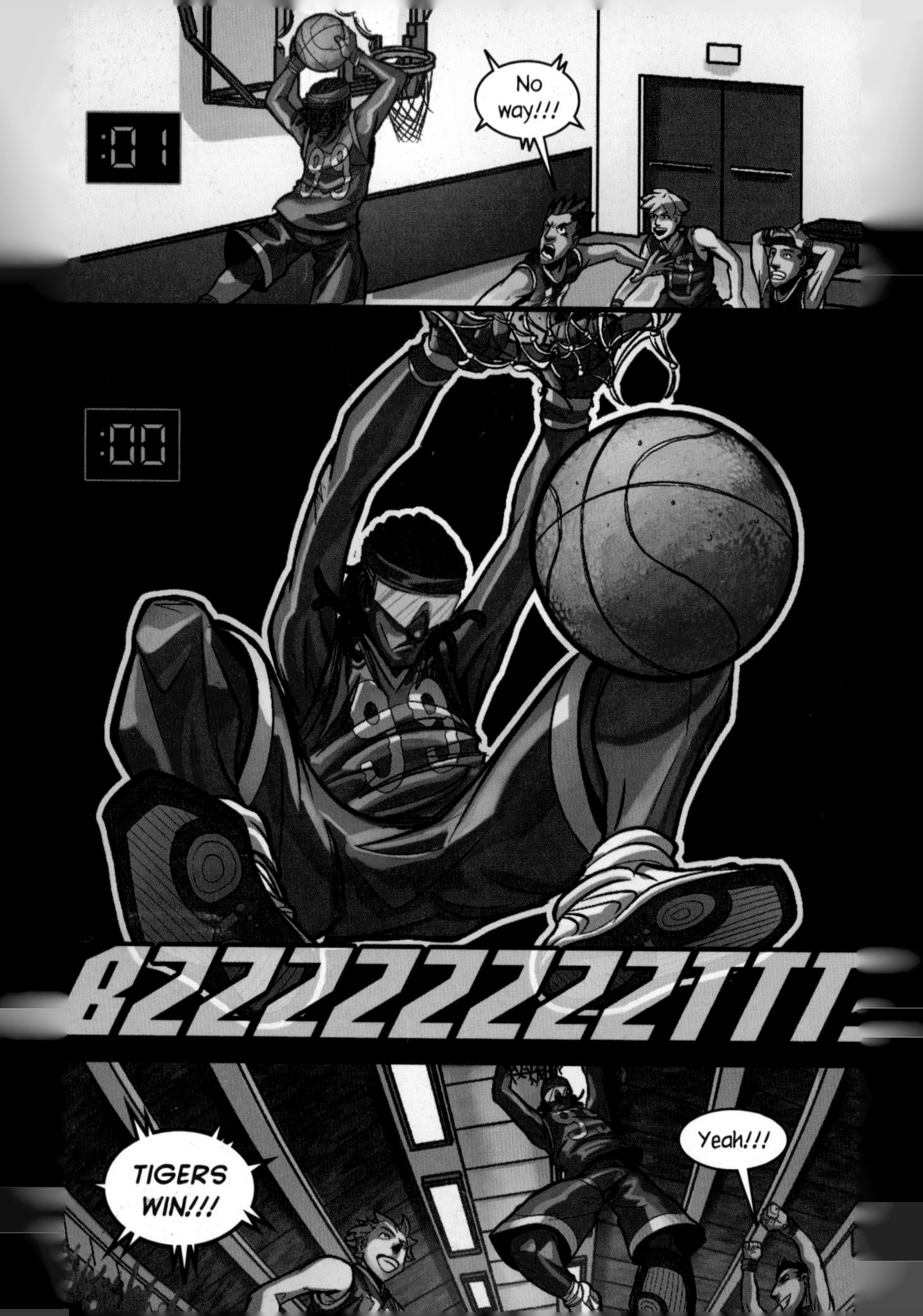
:01
No way!!!
:00
BZZZZZZZZZTTT
TIGERS WIN!!!
Yeah!!!

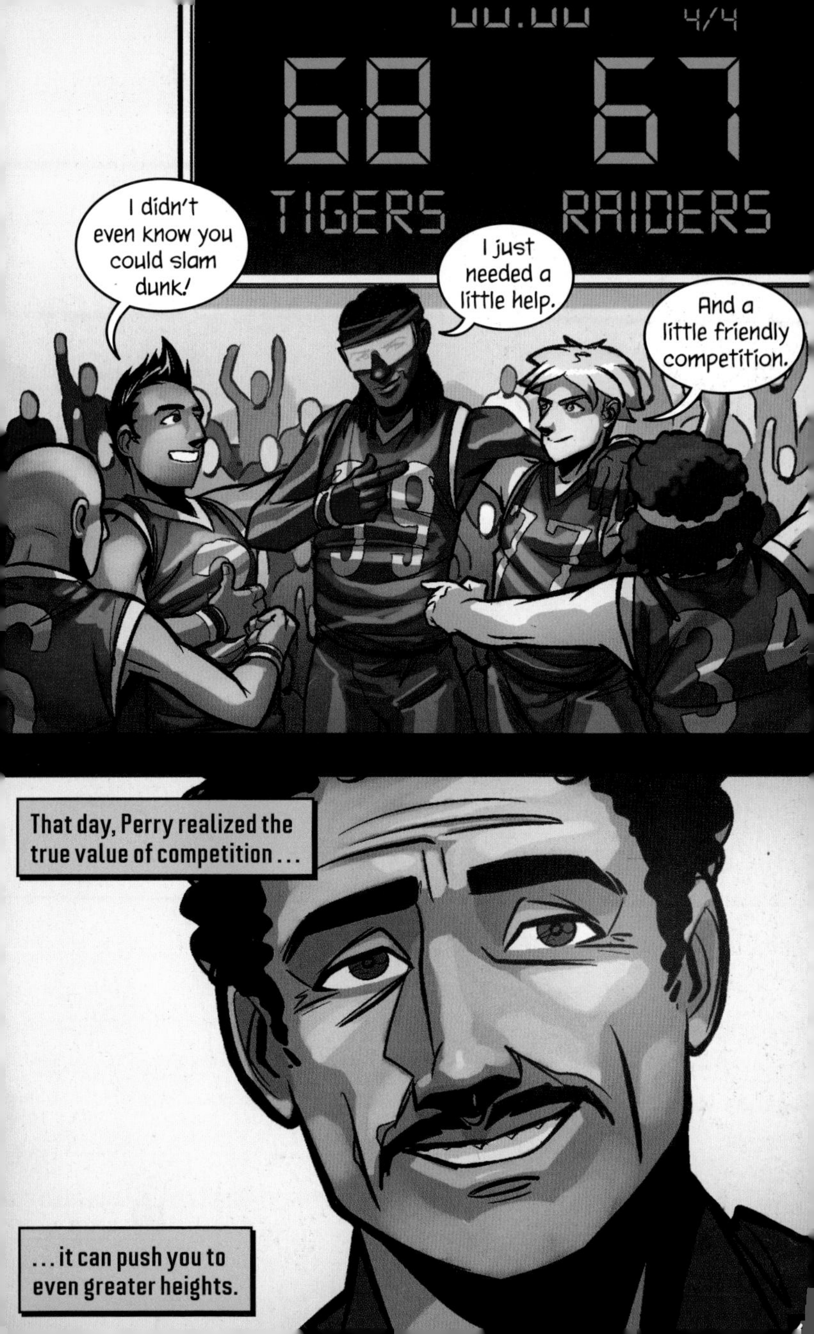
TIGERS
68
RAIDERS
67
4/4
I didn't even know you could slam dunk!
I just needed a little help.
And a little friendly competition.
That day, Perry realized the true value of competition . . .
. . . it can push you to even greater heights.

SPORTS ZONE
POSTGAME RECAP

BBL
BASKETBALL

PNT
PAINTBALL

FBL
FOOTBALL

BSL
BASEBALL

SOC
SOCCER

HKY

CARTER

TIGERS BAND TOGETHER FOR THRILLING VICTORY AGAINST RAIDERS

TIGERS   RAIC

BY THE NUMBERS

POINTS:
BOYD: 23
CARTER: 19

ASSISTS:
KADIR: 14
BOYD: 7

STORY: The ultra-talented Tigers finally found their rhythm as they pounced on the Raiders and took home a big win. "Oohs" and "Ahhs" filled the air as Kadir made assists left and right, helping Perry and Jason sink bucket after bucket. In a big finish, all eyes were on the skies as Jason Carter soared above the rim to slam down a beautiful alley-oop pass from Perry Boyd.

Sports Illustrated KIDS

UP NEXT: SI KIDS INFO CENTER

SZ POSTGAME EXTRA

WHERE *YOU* ANALYZE THE GAME!

BLZ vs BKS 3-1
TGR vs RDR 33-32
EAG vs BAN 14-7
SPA vs WLD 4-3
BAN vs RDR 21-15
RZR vs LIG 4-3

Basketball fans got a real treat today when the Tigers one-upped the former state champs, the Raiders, in a close game. Let's go into the bleachers and ask some fans for their thoughts on the day's events . . .

DISCUSSION QUESTION 1

Which position is the hardest to play — center, point guard, or shooting guard? Why?

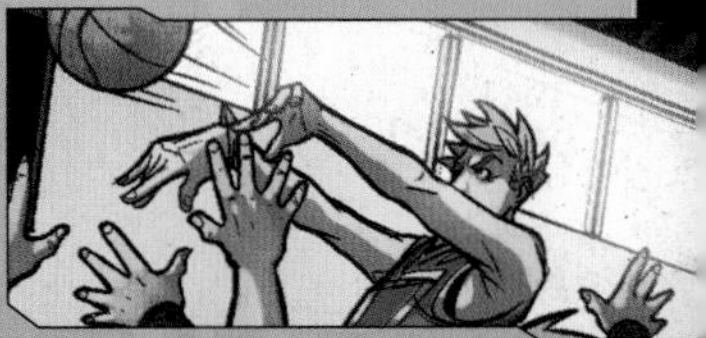

DISCUSSION QUESTION 2

Who was your favorite player — Kadir Amad, Jason Carter, or Perry Boyd?

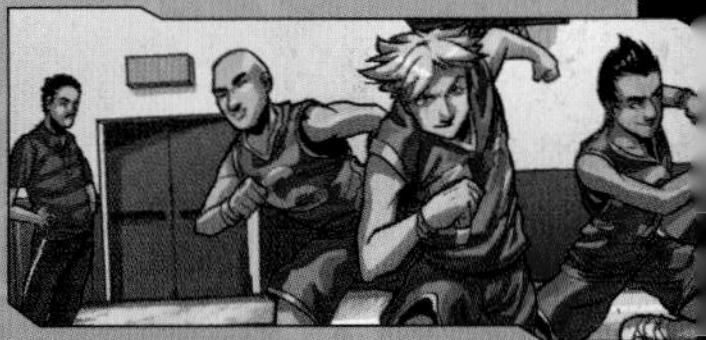

WRITING PROMPT 1

Has your family had to move? What do you think is the hardest part about changing schools? What are the best ways to make new friends? Write about it.

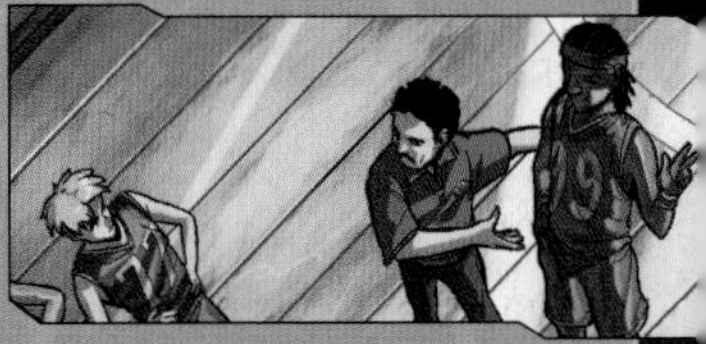

WRITING PROMPT 2

Perry and Jason hook up to make an awesome play to win the game. Think up your own play from beginning to end. Then draw out your play with X's and O's .

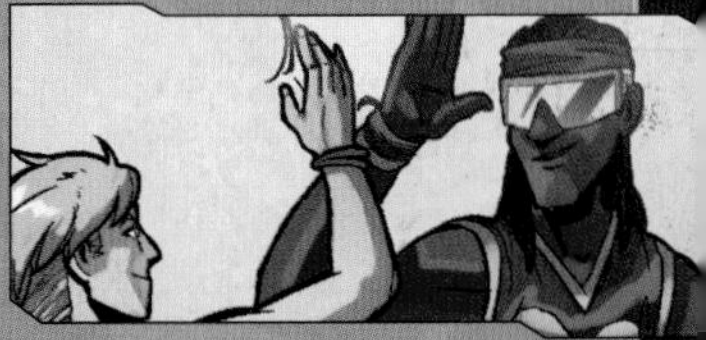

GLOSSARY

CENTER (SEN-tur)—a position played by a tall team member who plays mostly under the rim

COMPETITION (kom-puh-TISH-uhn)—a contest of some kind, or when two or more people are trying to get the same thing

OPPOSITION (op-uh-ZISH-uhn)—the person or team that you play against in a competition or game

PICK AND ROLL (PIK AND ROHL)—a play where one teammate sets a pick to free up a second teammate. Then, that same teammate moves around the pick for a return pass.

POINT GUARD (POINT GAHRD)—a quick player who handles the ball and runs a team's offensive plays

SCRIMMAGE (SKRIM-ij)—a game played for practice

SHOOTING GUARD (SHOO-ting GAHRD)—a shooting guard's main responsibility is to score points

THRIVES (THRIVEZ)—does well and flourishes

CREATORS

CHRIS KREIE › *Author*

Chris Kreie lives in Minnesota with his wife and two children. He works as a school librarian, and writes books like this one in his free time.

ABURTOV › *Illustrator*

Aburtov is a graphic designer and illustrator who has worked in the comic book industry for more than 11 years. In that time, Aburtov has colored popular characters like Wolverine, Iron Man, Punisher, and Blade. He recently created his own studio called Graphikslava. Aburtov lives with his beloved wife in Monterrey, Mexico, where he enjoys spending time with family and friends.

ANDRES ESPARZA › *Inker*

Andres Esparza has been a graphic designer, colorist, and illustrator for many different companies and agencies. Andres now works as a full-time artist for Graphikslava studio in Monterrey, Mexico. In his spare time, Andres loves to play basketball, hang out with family and friends, and listen to good music.

FARES MAESE › *Colorist*

Fares Maese is a graphic designer and illustrator. He has worked as a colorist for Marvel Comics, and as a concept artist for the card and role-playing games Pathfinder and Warhammer. Fares loves spending time playing video games with his Graphikslava comrades, and he's an awesome drum player.

Sports Illustrated KIDS GRAPHIC NOVELS
QUICK COMIC

ZACK FULLER and PERRY BOYD IN:

FULL COURT PRESSURE

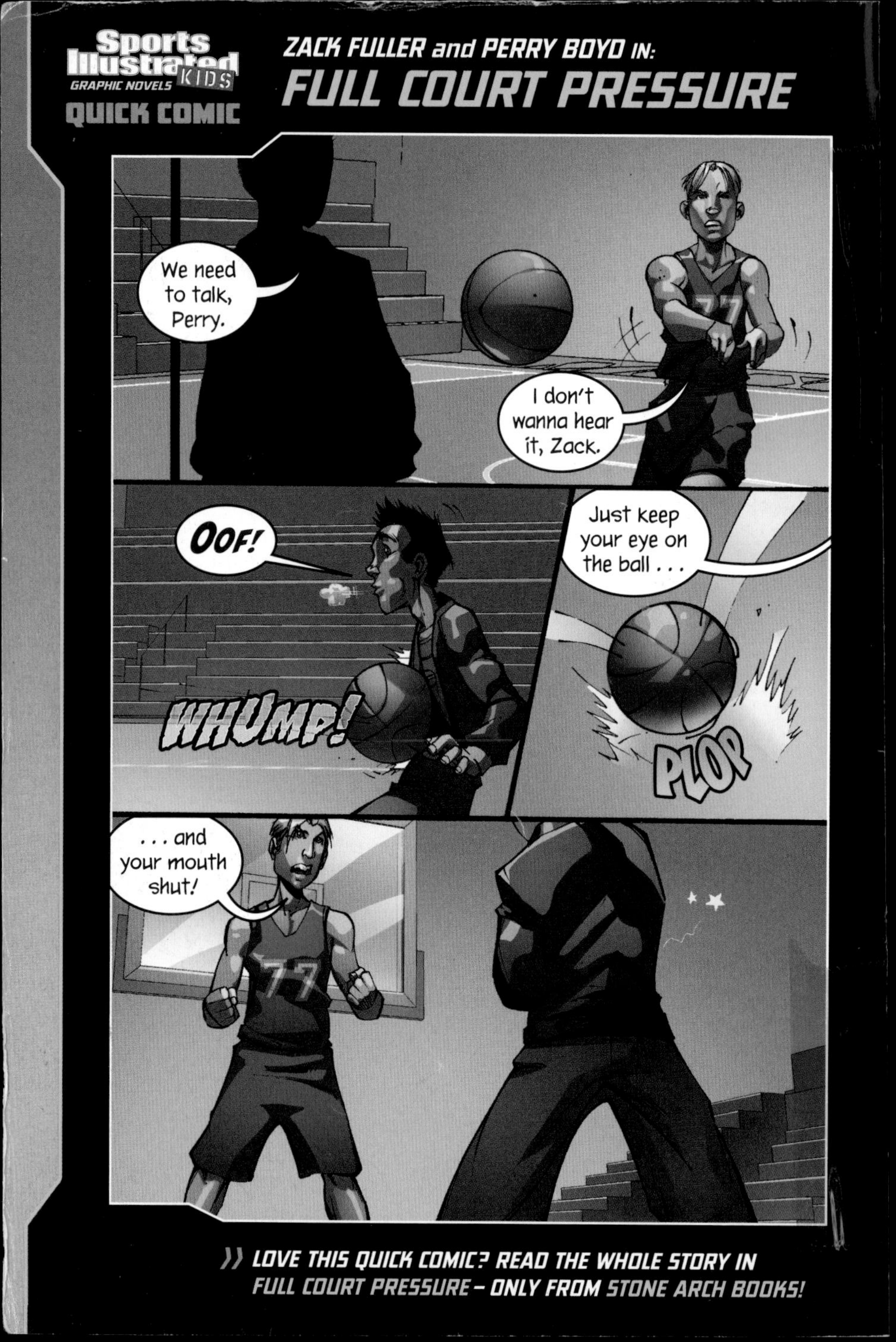
We need to talk, Perry.
I don't wanna hear it, Zack.
OOF!
WHUMP!
Just keep your eye on the ball . . .
PLOP
. . . and your mouth shut!

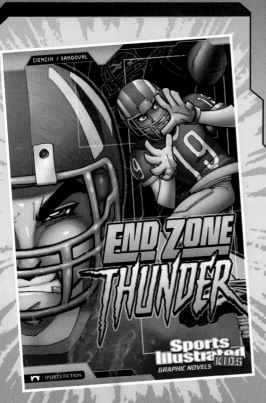

WAIT!

DON'T CLOSE THE BOOK!
THERE'S MORE!

FIND MORE:
GAMES
PUZZLES
CHARACTERS

www.capstonekids.com

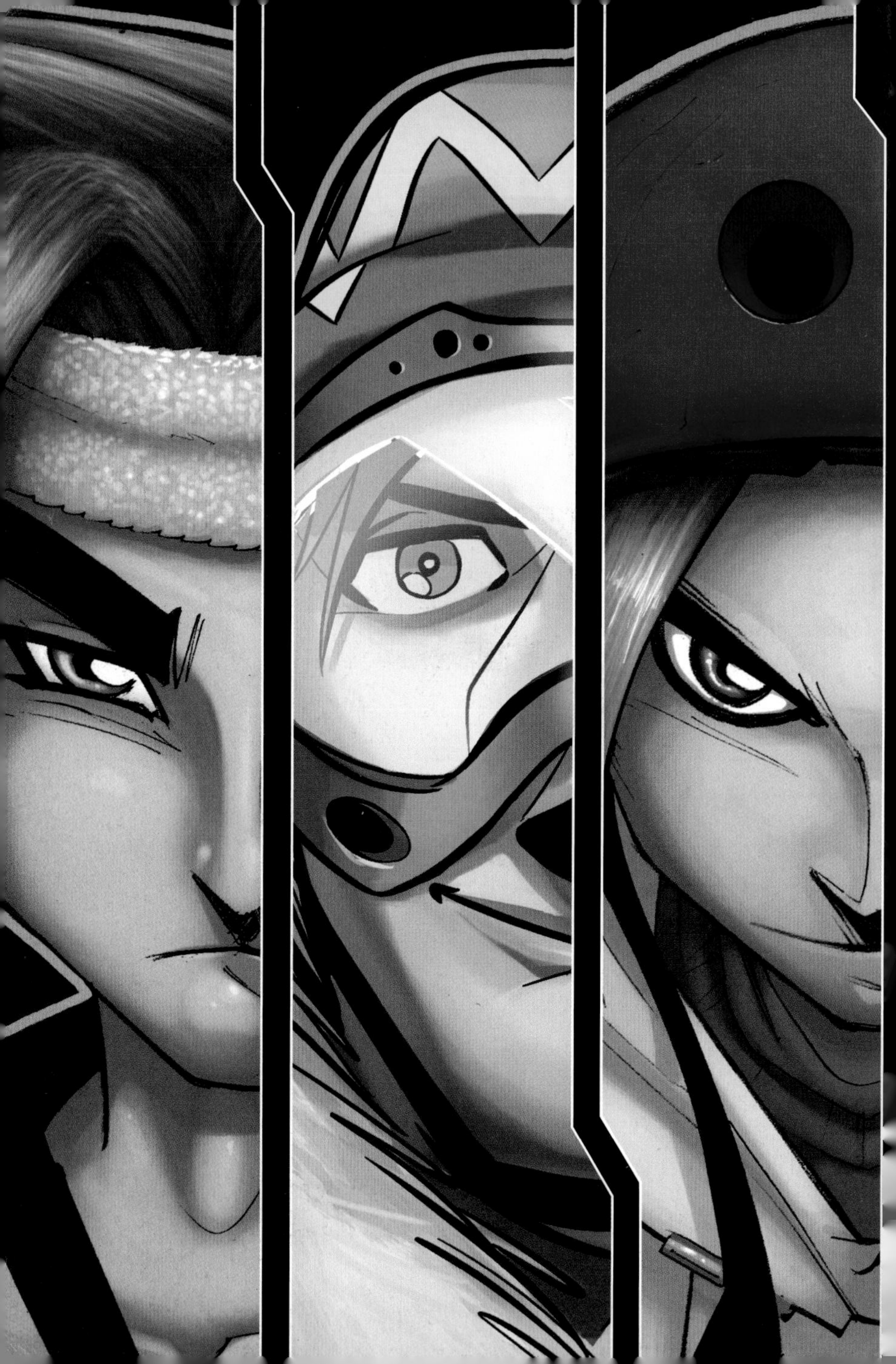

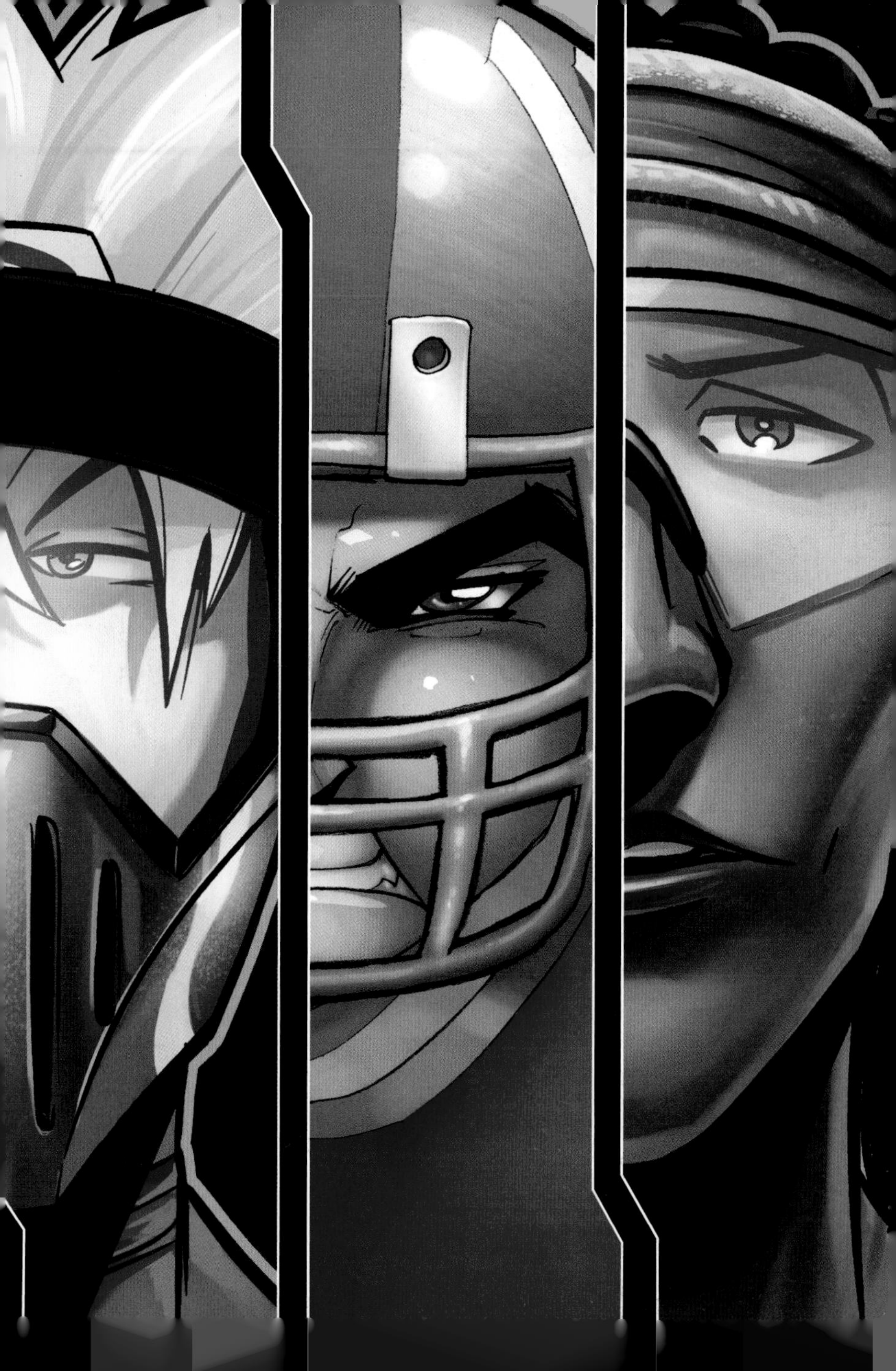

Sports Illustrated KIDS

GRAPHIC NOVELS

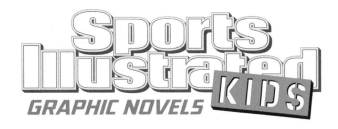

STONE ARCH BOOKS